*Erica began weeping loudly into her pillow as soon as James had left the cabin, her sobs obliterating all other sounds. So by the time she realized what was happening, he was already halfway across the bedroom to her. . . .*

"I can't take this anymore!" he shouted fiercely, grabbing her by both arms and pulling her off the bed.

Erica gasped, "I didn't mean for you to hear—"

"I don't care what might happen later. I can't stand seeing you like this, and I can't stand myself like this. Do you want me, Red? Do you want me to stay?"

She looked at James in stark amazement. "What did you say?"

"I'm half out of my mind from wanting you." He pulled her closer and searched her eyes. "No promises, no regrets, Erica. Just you and me." His voice dropped to a gravelly whisper. "Do you want me to love you?"

Dreams came true, magic was real, and for the first time in her life, she belonged.

"Oh, *yes.* . . ."

## WHAT ARE *LOVESWEPT* ROMANCES?

They are stories of true romance and touching emotion. We believe those two very important ingredients are constants in our highly sensual and very believable stories in the *LOVESWEPT* line. Our goal is to give you, the reader, stories of consistently high quality that may sometimes make you laugh, sometimes make you cry, but are always fresh and creative and contain many delightful surprises within their pages.

Most romance fans read an enormous number of books. Those they truly love, they keep. Others may be traded with friends and soon forgotten. We hope that each *LOVESWEPT* romance will be a treasure—a "keeper." We will always try to publish

*LOVE STORIES YOU'LL NEVER FORGET*
*BY AUTHORS YOU'LL ALWAYS REMEMBER*

The Editors

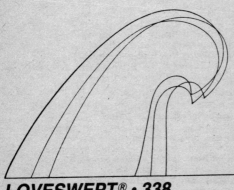

LOVESWEPT® • 338

# Deborah Smith
# The Cherokee Trilogy:
# Tempting the Wolf

 BANTAM BOOKS
NEW YORK • TORONTO • LONDON • SYDNEY • AUCKLAND

*TEMPTING THE WOLF*

*A Bantam Book / July 1989*

If you would be interested in receiving protective vinyl
covers for your Loveswept books, please write to this address
for information:

*Loveswept*
*Bantam Books*
*P.O. Box 985*
*Hicksville, NY 11802*

ISBN 0-553-22012-8

# *Prologue*

Katherine Blue Song made her way out of the huge Cherokee camp, dimly aware of the glances of the soldiers stationed around the perimeter. She knew they didn't care if one less scrawny, sick Indian survived the march to the Western territory.

She staggered when her worn moccasins let frozen clumps of snow torment feet that were already chapped raw, but the fever kept her from shivering. Physical discomfort faded along with her hope for survival, and she wished for only two things—that she could tell Justis Gallatin how much she loved him, and that she could be buried beside her family in Georgia.

*Someday I'll go back there.* The promise had kept her spirits up for months, but it was folly to believe it now.

Disoriented from sickness and hunger, Katherine wasn't certain how far she walked along the high bluffs overlooking the Mississippi River. She dropped her frayed blanket on a snowy knoll, then sank down on it and draped her hair around her shoulders as a little protection from the cold. The thin linsey-woolsey dress she wore was a far cry from the fine gowns Justis had insisted on giving her.

Tears filled her eyes as she gazed at the broad, ice-filled river. Under a full moon, the ice shimmered like the crystal chandelier her mother had hung in the dining room back home. Too fancy for a farmhouse, her father had said teasingly, but the Blue Songs were prosperous, proud farmers, like many of their Cherokee relatives.

The chandelier hadn't survived the white mob who attacked after the state militia came.

*I'll buy you a dozen chandeliers,* Justis had told her later, gruffly trying to be kind.

*Justis.* Katherine lifted her face to the moon and gazed woozily into its pale light. "I wish he had loved me," she whispered.

"Her name is Katlanicha Blue Song," Justis Gallatin told the grim-faced Cherokee matron. "But she goes by the name Katherine, too. I just want to find her. I don't mean the gal no harm."

He squatted by the campfire and pushed a wide-brimmed hat back from his face so that the woman could study the honesty in his eyes.

She stared hard into their green depths, then studied his chestnut hair and frowned at his moustache. Finally she scowled at the luxury of his heavy fur coat and warm wool scarf. Without hesitation he pulled the scarf off and handed it to her. She ignored the gift.

"You call her 'Beloved Woman,' " Justis said, speaking slowly so that she'd understand his poor Cherokee. "Everyone on the trail has heard of her. She knows white medicine and white ways."

"I hear nothing of such a one." The old woman stirred hominy gruel in a chipped kettle set on the embers at the fire's edge. "Go away."

No one was talking. They didn't trust him, and so they protected Katherine. He understood why they loved her—Lord, how he understood. If only Katie had believed that no one, Indian or white, could love her more than he did.

Justis stood wearily, his shoulders slumped. He was

a strong, no-nonsense man, used to hardship and self-denial, but tonight he was nearly beaten by the fear and fatigue that had swallowed him during the months since Katherine's disappearance. Dully he noticed a lanky young Cherokee man hurrying toward the campfire.

"Mother!" he exclaimed in Cherokee. "The Beloved Woman won't eat! And she's gone to walk beside the river alone!"

The woman gasped. "Be quiet!"

Justis ran for his horses. Behind him he heard the woman yelling for help.

Katherine swayed as a gust of wind hit her. She leaned forward, placed both hands on the blanket, and braced her arms. Five-foot-long strands of thick black hair floated behind her as she tilted her face up even more toward the high, cold moon. She could feel its silver fingers running over her.

This same moon was shining on Georgia, blessing the graves of the parents and sisters who kept watch over Blue Song land. Katherine's head swam, and she shook it groggily. Somehow, some way, that land would always belong to her family, even if Justis produced a thousand deeds bearing his title to it.

She cried out sadly. Justis Gallatin had become part of her soul, but he'd never own her, any more than he owned the land in Gold Ridge. Some things had to be won through love, and love alone.

At first she didn't hear the repetitive thudding of horses' hooves racing up the slope to her sitting place. When she did, she lurched to her feet. Katherine staggered, then caught her balance and looked wildly toward the sound.

The moon silhouetted the dark figures of a tall rider and two big horses. The horses were only a few strides away, and they were charging directly toward her. The rider reached out in her direction.

The horse's shoulder bumped her, and she nearly fell

down. When Katherine felt the rider's hand winding into the neck of her dress, she began to claw at him and struggle.

"Katie, girl, calm down!"

*Justis.* Stunned, she stopped fighting, and he pulled her onto the saddle in front of him. His long arm went around her waist like an iron band.

She sagged groggily against him, her hands digging into the wide, furry wall of his coat, her face burrowed in his shoulder. Her feverish mind knew only that hope had come back into the world, and she couldn't understand the distant sounds of men shouting and horses' hooves racing in muffled rhythms. Justis held her tighter and clucked to his horses. They went into a smooth, rocking lope following the riverbank north.

Katherine tilted her head back and tried to look at Justis in the moonlit darkness. Love overwhelmed her, until all she could manage to say was a plaintive, "Home?"

He bent his head close to hers, brushed a kiss over her forehead, and whispered, "Someday."

# *One*

Okay, so she was probably the only Cherokee who had red hair, green eyes, and skin that bypassed fair and went straight to paleface.

Erica Gallatin stared at herself in the gilt-edged mirror of her hotel room and doggedly searched for some hint of her Indian blood. She finally settled for the fact that her cheekbones were high and her nose had a noble ridge that some people kindly referred to as distinctive.

Distinctive, yes. Not pretty—but who needed pretty, when she had distinctive? Under *distinctive* in the dictionary it read, "Clearly marking a person or thing as different from others."

Well, then, she'd be one helluva different Cherokee.

Carrying a sturdy ballpoint pen—none of that frivolous felt-tipped stuff for her—and a leather folder embossed with "Gallatin Construction" in plain white letters, Erica left her room and went downstairs.

"Good timbers," she murmured aloud, and pressed the toe of one practical blue pump into the oak planks of the foyer floor. She had enormous respect for anything built to last, and the Kirkland Inn dated back to 1835. It was, in fact, the oldest building in Gold Ridge, Georgia, a town that preserved everything about its heritage from the gold-rush days.

Erica gazed at a wall covered with framed photographs that illustrated the progress of Gold Ridge from rowdy frontier town to charming tourist mecca. The oldest was dated 1850, and there were no Cherokees to be seen, since the Indians had been forced to move west in 1838.

"We're baaack," she sang under her breath, and, feeling proud, headed for the inn's dining room.

Her cousins had already come downstairs and were sipping tea from pink china cups. Correction. Tess Gallatin was sipping, one little finger arched delicately in her best English-boarding-school tradition. Kat Gallatin held her cup like a can of beer.

Erica stopped at the door before they saw her, and took a moment to gaze at them with renewed awe. Their corner table was framed by a large window and curtains of white eyelet. Golden afternoon light filtered across their faces, and a late-blooming dogwood tree feathered its white blossoms against the window as if eager to draw their attention. Because their branches of the Gallatin family had married back into the tribe, Kat was nearly full-blooded Cherokee, and Tess was half. They looked wonderfully exotic despite the fact that Tess wore a flowing turquoise dress straight out of a Beverly Hills designer collection and Kat wore jeans and a road-race T-shirt.

Erica sighed with nostalgia for a heritage she'd never known and approached the table with quick, determined strides. "Hello, cousins."

They looked up expectantly, and both smiled. "Just in time. We ordered another pot of tea," Tess said in a lilting British accent.

Kat impishly arched one black brow and raised a hand. "How."

Erica sat down slowly, gazing at Kat in surprise. "Doesn't that kind of Tonto talk offend you?"

Kat shrugged. "Nope. Seems harmless to me. I've never felt like an Indian."

"Nor have I," Tess added. "Not after being raised in England by Swedish grandparents."

Erica put her folder down, straightened her gray, pin-striped skirt and jacket with quick little tugs, and said wistfully, "I'm only one-sixteenth Cherokee. If you guys don't feel like Indians, is there any hope for me?"

Tess laughed gently and Kat grinned. "We've all got a lot to learn," Kat said. "Let's get to it. I have to be in New Orleans by tonight. Princess Talana is wrestling Big Bad Mama, and I need the money."

"And I have to meet with a wholesaler in L.A. tomorrow morning," Tess added.

Erica shook her head in amused delight. Tess was a diamond broker, and Kat, petite, adorable Kat, was a wrestler. "Princess Talana. Is that your professional name?"

"Uh-huh. I'm the noble Indian maiden. That bit."

Erica sighed and opened her folder. "I wrote down everything we learned from the lawyer this morning, and I had copies made of all the documents."

"My word, you're efficient," Tess said with admiration.

"I'm the old-maid businesswoman in this trio. Fits my image." She riffled through the papers and handed them out. "Copies of our land plot, of Dove Gallatin's will, and of the personal data we were told about. I'll read that aloud, and you guys tell me if I made any mistakes."

Erica snapped the paper and cleared her throat. "We share the same great-great-grandparents, Justis and Katherine Gallatin; their sons were our great-grand-fathers. Mine was Ross Gallatin, whom I know nothing about; Kat's was Holt Gallatin—"

"The bank robber," Kat noted proudly.

"And Tess's was Silas Gallatin, who owned a ship-ping business in San Francisco."

"That's all I know about him," Tess interjected.

Erica nodded. "We were all born on the same day, September 27, but in different years. Kat is twenty-eight, divorced, and lives in Miami; Tess is twenty-six, widowed, and lives in Long Beach, California; and yours truly is an ancient thirty-three, never been married, and lives in Washington, D.C., where she builds yuppie houses."

"That last one sounds interesting," Tess noted. "Tell us more."

Erica smiled ruefully. "My branch of the Gallatin family left the reservation decades ago and turned into plain old Anglo-Saxons. The most exciting thing we've ever done is vote Independent and refuse to wear white gloves at garden parties."

"Better than growing up in the circus," Kat interjected. "And spending your life on the road. I envy you."

"I envy *you*. And Tess. Tess lives on a sailboat."

"We each envy the other," Tess remarked. "I think it's lovely that we feel so close even though we've just met."

Erica looked at her cousins affectionately. "It's the Indian blood. It's a bond."

"Whoo, she's being mystical," Kat said teasingly.

Tess smiled. "Perhaps we'll all feel that way once we investigate our branches of the Gallatin family."

Erica pulled a heavy gold medallion from a pocket of her skirt. "Which brings us to these." Tess and Kat produced their own medallions, each covered with a winding circle of Cherokee symbols on both sides. "Why did Dove Gallatin leave two hundred acres of Gold Ridge land to three relatives she'd never met? And why did she specify which of us gets each medallion?"

"They have different symbols," Tess noted.

Kat lovingly caressed her medallion. "Do you think our great-great-grandparents made these? Maybe the gold came from the land here."

"It was Katherine Gallatin's land. Cherokee land," Tess said. "She made certain it would always stay in the family. I believe the gold *did* come from here."

Erica felt a heaviness in her chest as she thought of the magnificent valley and forests the lawyer had shown them. "Which brings us to the next point. We'd be smart to lease the land to Tri-State Mining."

"I need the money, but I hate to think what they'd do to the land," Kat murmured.

"It's beautiful," Tess agreed. "I know we should be practical, but . . ."

"I've been practical all my life." Erica looked at her cousins solemnly. "In this case I hate to be practical." They nodded. "So before we make a decision about the land, we go back to our respective homes and see what we can learn about our Gallatin history. Still agreed on that point?"

"Yes, most certainly," Tess said.

"You bet," Kat chimed in.

They placed their medallions on the table and studied them raptly. Each was punched with a hole, so that it could be hung on a necklace, and each bore at least a century's worth of nicks and rubbed spots. They had been well loved and much worn.

Erica tingled inside with the mystery of it all. She spread her hands over the medallions and traded determined looks with her newfound cousins. "These medallions mean something," she told them softly. "And we have to find out what it is."

A blur of movement made the three of them turn toward the window. A bluebird perched in the dogwood tree, singing as if with approval.

What the hell was he doing there? And what difference did it make?

James Tall Wolf leaned against a wall outside the opulent banquet room, one expensively loafered foot crossed over the other, big-knuckled hands shoved in the pockets of custom-tailored trousers, an unlit cigar clenched between his teeth.

He asked himself the same questions every time he spoke at one of these shindigs, and lately it had been at least once a month. Was he just a curiosity, or did these business types really listen? How could he make them listen? Should he just tell them to go suck a totem pole, that Indians didn't need their smug patronage?

"Mr. Tall Wolf! I've been looking for you!"

James glanced down the hall. The little blonde was so close that he could see her eyelashes flutter invitingly. Her gaze lingered on his face as if she'd never seen such fascinating features. He straightened and put his cigar in his shirt pocket.

"Mr. Tall Wolf," she said sweetly, and held out a hand. "Let me show you to your table. I'm Lisa, the publicity coordinator for the developers' association. We're so glad to have you as a speaker. You're such a credit to your people."

James smiled at her, shook hands, and felt her forefingers stroke his palm. *Credit to your people.* Okay, he wouldn't tell her how insulting that line was. He'd learned long ago that there was no tactful way to explain without coming across as arrogant and oversensitive, neither of which did the tribe's image any good.

"Why, thank you," he said drolly. "It's not true that the only good Indian is a dead Indian."

She laughed. "Oh, it's so nice to see that you have a sense of humor about yourself." She caressed his arm through the sleeves of his dark jacket as they walked into the ballroom of the hotel. "Do you get back to D.C. often, these days?"

"Every few months. I've got some real-estate investments here."

"I'm a big Redskins fan."

*In more way than one*, James thought wryly. "Thank you."

"I was sorry when you retired."

"I was too. But I like to walk without limping."

"You look very healthy. Very." She led him between banquet tables that were quickly filling with members of the developers' association. "Do you ever see your old teammates?"

"Occasionally. I've been away from pro ball for three years, though."

"Which reservation do you live on? The one in Oklahoma or in North Carolina?"

"Neither. I've got a little piece of land in Virginia."

She looked surprised. "But I thought—"

"That all Indians lived on reservations." He smiled wickedly. "I'm a renegade."

"Yum. I'd love to see your teepee some time."

"It's not called a teepee. And it's not much to see."

"I'm free this weekend."

"Sorry. I've already accepted an invitation to a scalping party."

"You like blond hair?" She pulled a strand of hers over one eye and winked at him. "Think of the delicious contrasts we could make."

"I'm color-blind."

She laughed playfully. "Hair color isn't important from the waist down."

They reached the table on the dais and stopped. James shook her hand in farewell. Again he felt the slow, intimate movement of her fingertip in his palm. He sighed. "Lisa, I only sleep with Indian women."

She jabbed him with her nail. "You're kidding!"

"Nope. There's only so much of me to go around. I have to serve my people every chance I get."

She studied his slitted eyes, frowned, and suddenly seemed grateful to introduce him to the association's president, so that she could end her responsibilities.

James sat down next to the president and distractedly exchanged greetings with him and the other men at the head table. His thoughts churned. Once upon a time he would have encouraged the blonde's attention and heartily enjoyed the result.

Now he understood that he was an exotic pet to many women; through him they could fulfill some harmless Wild West fantasies about Indians, he guessed. He was good at giving them what they wanted, but he didn't get enough in return anymore.

*I'm getting old and cranky,* he told himself as he ate his salad. His bad knee ached more often than it used to, and he missed his family down in North Carolina more than ever. He hadn't been home in four years, and, homesick as he was now, still he remembered funerals and bitterness.

"The ugly ones always make trouble."

"You think she's ugly?"

"She's six feet tall, for cryin' out loud! Women that big are always insecure. They don't feel feminine, so they end up trying to dominate men."

James forgot his brooding and listened curiously as his dinner partners continued to whisper among themselves.

"You don't know Ricky, or you wouldn't say that."

The heavyset man to James's left snorted derisively. "The broad stole that award from me last year."

"Stole it? Hell. She earned that construction award."

"Well, she sure didn't sleep with anybody to get it. Not unless one of the judges liked big-mouthed, skinny broads."

Intrigued, James looked around for the troublesome Ricky.

"Excuse me. Thank you. Sorry I'm late." The tall woman slipped awkwardly between nearby tables, bumping people with a scuffed brown briefcase.

She was gawky in an endearing sort of way; not clumsy, exactly, but all arms and legs, in a blue skirt and jacket that were too plain and a little too big. Her wavy, shoulder-length chestnut hair was laughably disheveled, but it reflected the overhead lights in glossy coppers and golds that held James's rapt gaze.

No one would ever call this woman pretty, not in the soft, rounded way of most women, but no man in his right mind would call that combination of statuesque body, glorious hair, and beautifully chiseled face *ugly*.

She drew glances from many in the nearly all-male crowd, and the red dots on her cheeks told James that she was painfully uncomfortable with the attention. She scooted into a chair at a table right in front and sat there with rigid dignity. He could see her profile, and in it he read careful reserve. She was a successful woman in a profession dominated by men from the highest management to the lowest laborer, and she probably knew that she was an easy target for jealousy.

James studied the tentative, tight smile she offered her table mates. She was aware that her entrance had elicited everything from compliments to contempt. She was definitely an outsider.

*You and me both, doll,* James told her silently. A tingling sense of arousal came over him, a sudden affection and protectiveness. His body's response didn't surprise him, but the sentimentality did. He kept watching her in the hope she would look in his direction.

The man who'd defended her at James's table turned around and called, "Hey, Ricky, leave the killer briefcase at the office next time."

She swiveled, looked relieved to see a friendly face, and patted the bulky leather rectangle by her ankles. "I was out at a site, and my truck died. I took a cab. And I have to go back to the office after dinner."

"All work and no play, Ricky," he said teasingly.

The heavyset man snickered. "She's not exactly a plaything. I'd rather make it with a construction crane."

"You know," James told him in a soft, pleasant tone, "one of the most distinguishing things about Cherokee culture has always been its respect for women. Cherokee women could fight in battle and hold positions of power on the councils. And the family structure was a matriarchy. When a man married, he became part of his wife's clan. My name, for example. Tall Wolf. That originated with my female ancestors in the wolf clan."

"That's why our soldiers were able to kick the Indians' butts." The man slapped his thigh and guffawed. "The squaws were in charge while the braves lay around."

A waiter placed a thick steak in front of James. James studied it for a moment, wondering idly how it would look flattened on his table mate's face. "Former Redskin wallops jackass with beef. Details at eleven." No, it would play too big in the media.

"Some of us don't use those terms," James explained

patiently. "Squaw, brave, buck, papoose—they're considered demeaning stereotypes. They're descriptions white people created. They keep us out of the mainstream."

"Don't tell me you people are into all that consciousness raising, affirmative-action stuff. You're a businessman, just like me. You know that all this minority bellyaching is ruining us."

James's frayed patience dissolved in one blistering second of anger. The depth of that anger startled him, but he knew he had nothing to fear from it. In the old days, when he was out of control, he would have thrown a plateful of steak in the man's face, and probably his fist, too.

He glanced up and saw the skinny redhead gazing at him anxiously. The look in her eyes was so worried that he stared back at her, shocked that a stranger had deciphered his mood.

James was a master at returning flirtations, but this was no flirtation. This was compassion. He lost himself in her soulful green eyes.

"What about that issue, James?" the obnoxious questioner asked. "Are you people big on federal handout programs?"

James turned slowly to the man. "We're big on anything that helps us keep what's left of our land and culture." He tossed his napkin on the table and told the association president, "Come get me when you need me. I'll be in the hall."

He stood and walked out of the room. Even in his anger it seemed to James that he could feel the redhead's eyes on him as he left.

There had to be a bond between people with Cherokee blood, Erica thought. Why else would James Tall Wolf have returned her gaze so intensely and with such gratitude?

She could barely eat. Where had he gone? What had

that jerk, Harold Brumby, said to him? Harold a hulking Archie Bunker type, as sensitive as a log, was constantly in trouble with some union or other.

James Tall Wolf. The moment she'd learned that he was the guest speaker at the association's spring meeting she'd rearranged her schedule so she could attend. For years she'd heard of the Cherokee Indian who played defense for the Washington Redskins.

The press always made a big joke out of the coincidence—an Indian Redskin—but, not being a football fan, she'd never paid much attention. And after all, James Tall Wolf had left professional football three years ago, owing to a knee problem.

From now on, she'd pay attention.

She tuned in to the conversation at her table.

"He's off the juice, you can tell. I bet he's dropped thirty pounds since he retired."

"You know that stuff turns 'em into monsters. It makes 'em big and mean."

"Wolfman was one of the meanest. I swear, I think his own teammates were afraid of him sometimes. But he was great."

"The coaches like that, when the guys are half crazy. It's a big macho thing. Everybody thought it was funny when the Wolfman used to tear up benches with his bare hands."

The men chuckled among themselves. Erica sat there feeling a little stunned. "What's juice?" she asked. "Alcohol?"

"Steroids," one of the men explained. "Growth hormones." He growled comically. "Testosterone."

"Ah." James Tall Wolf didn't look as though he needed any extra of that. "Aren't steroids dangerous?"

"Sure. But a lot of the guys in pro football take them. Makes 'em play better."

"Defensive linemen are animals anyway," someone added. "Gorillas in helmets."

Erica poked nervously at her food. She'd made eye contact with a dangerous man, then. Funny, he'd looked gentle. There was something exciting about being noticed by a man who tore up benches with his bare hands.

She waited anxiously for him to come back into the room; finally, during dessert, he did. Erica had hoped to study every fascinating detail of him, but as soon as he appeared his gaze went straight to hers.

She clutched the napkin in her lap. What had she done to deserve this scrutiny? She knew how to deal with brawny, aggressive men—over the years she'd turned a few obnoxious construction workers into little piles of chewed hide—but she didn't want anyone nicknamed Wolfman mad at her. Frowning, she turned her attention to a piece of runny lime pie and ate as if it were delicious.

But every time she glanced up, he was still watching her. Her stomach twisted. She knew she'd made a gawky entrance. That must be it—Harold Brumby had probably made fun of her, as she knew he'd done frequently since she'd won the construction award away from him.

Perhaps Harold had told some disgusting lie, and it had made James Tall Wolf find her fascinating, like a bizarre story in a grocery-store tabloid.

"Martians Disguised as Female Housebuilders. Two-Headed Hammers Discovered!"

She made certain her pie lasted until the association's president got up and welcomed James as the guest speaker. Erica kept her attention on the last crumbs as she listened carefully to the introduction. Honors and awards as a star player for North Carolina State—the Wolfman had played for the N.C. State Wolfpack (hah-hah)—then many more as a defensive lineman for the Redskins (hah-hah); and now James Tall Wolf was a successful entrepreneur, with varied investments in real estate.

And to top it all off, as the president pointed out, James was a full-blooded Cherokee, who devoted much of his spare time to telling his inspirational story to groups all over the country. He was a splendid example of the American Indian's progress.

Erica winced. The president implied that Indian culture was backward, though she was certain the man hadn't intended any insult. How did James put up with such misguided, patronizing attitudes?

*Give 'em hell, Tall Wolf,* she thought proudly. As everyone applauded, Erica lifted her gaze to the podium and clapped vigorously.

The Wolfman was looking directly at her.

Erica's hands hesitated in midair. She felt like hiding her face from his persistent scrutiny, and her silliness horrified her.

She could do nothing but gaze back at him and wait to see what he'd do next. What he did was start talking in a deep, melodic voice faintly touched by a southern drawl; a voice so rich that it made her think of chocolate.

Finally he drew his gaze away from her to look at his audience. Erica sagged as if a puppeteer had let go of her strings.

Tall Wolf was perfection molded from bronze, his hair the color of sable, his eyes like dark mahogany. His features were classic—the high cheekbones, deep-set eyes, wide mouth, and blunt nose of a beautiful American original. Lord, get those male models off the cover, of Indian romances, put this man in their place, and sales would go sky-high.

Much like her pulse rate.

He had to be six-feet-four, at least, and his postfootball body was big but lean. He knew how to dress and obviously had the money to dress well; he wore a black sports coat, blue-gray pants, a crisp white shirt with a broadly spaced blue stripe, and a blue tie. A thick gold watch gleamed on his wrist.

"I took my grandfather to New York," he was telling the audience, "and we stood on Fifth Avenue during rush hour. We watched all the people for a while, and finally Grandfather turned to me and said, 'James, I don't think they're leaving.' "

The joke brought warm laughter and a smattering of applause. Erica felt a twinge of dismay. How could he make fun of such a sad subject? His people had lost so much over the years. She paused, thinking of the cousins she'd met two days before. *Our* people, she corrected herself, feeling proud.

"We Indians understand how tough it can be for you to accept us," Tall Wolf continued. "A few years ago we picketed the Bureau of Indian Affairs office, because we wanted more of our people in executive positions in the Bureau. An elderly lady walked up and gave us hell. 'If you don't like it in this country,' she said. 'why don't you go back where you came from?' "

Again the audience chortled. Again Erica cringed. What was James Tall Wolf, an Indian stand-up comic?

"We have a popular bumper sticker down on the reservation," he was saying. "It reads, 'I'm glad Columbus was looking for India instead of Turkey.' "

People guffawed and thumped the tables. Erica drummed her fingers and tried not to bite her tongue.

"We've made a great living at being mascots and advertising symbols," James told the audience. "Sports writers love us. 'Washington Redskins Scalp Opponents.' 'Cleveland Indians Go on Warpath.' Folks, we do take time out to pose in front of cigar stores, you know."

Erica couldn't stand it. He might come down from the podium and scalp her in revenge, but she had to say something. She stood up quickly. "Mr. Tall Wolf, could you tell us a little about some of the fine Indian leaders the Cherokees have had? Men like Sequoyah, who invented the Cherokee syllabary, and John Ross, who sued the federal government in an attempt to save the southern homelands?"

An awkward silence settled in the room. He stared at her for only a second. Then, an exasperated look on his face, he shot back, "I think you just told us."

Erica gritted her teeth as the audience chuckled at his quick reply. She didn't want to annoy him; she wanted to help. She kept her tone pleasant and sincere. "Do you feel that humor is an effective weapon against prejudice? Are the Cherokee people able to laugh about their problems the way you can?"

He bristled. "I'm not laughing at these problems."

"As their spokesman—"

"I'm just a businessman who happens to be Cherokee. I'm not the tribe's official representative."

"But you're treated that way. Is it a burden? Do you resent it?"

"This is a surprise," he said with a strained smile. "When I got here tonight I didn't notice the cameras from *Sixty Minutes*." Everyone laughed. "And you don't look like Mike Wallace."

Harold Brumby lolled back in his chair and said in a stage whisper, "Mike wears better suits."

No one dared laugh at that, but there were a lot of satisfied smiles. Erica felt a dull, sinking feeling at the center of her dignity, but she grinned cheerfully at Harold. "And Mike's a lot shorter."

Now the laughter was on her side. She glanced toward the podium and was surprised to see James Tall Wolf eyeing Harold with disgust. Slowly James swiveled his gaze to her.

"When you make people laugh *with* you about a problem, you gain their attention and respect," he told her. "I think you just proved that."

"Ah. Yes." She sat down, undone more by his subtle compliment than she would ever be by Harold's less-than-subtle insults.

He continued with his speech, but now he cast wary looks at her each time the audience laughed. Erica forced herself to smile and nod, but questions kept sticking in her throat. He wasn't addressing the issues.

At an opportune moment she vaulted to her feet. "Mr. Tall Wolf. Excuse me again."

The cuff of her jacket caught a spoon and sent it clattering loudly into her neighbor's coffee cup, splashing him. Erica grabbed the spoon and thunked it back into place, her face hot. *This is the closest I'll ever come to being a redskin,* she thought with silent humiliation.

"In the old days we named people according to their personalities," James Tall Wolf said in just the right tone of patronizing amusement. "I think I'll call you She-Who-Makes-Noise." He paused. "Okay, Noise, what is it now?"

Erica cleared her throat and waited for the chuckles to end. Damn him, he knew how to work a crowd. "Mr. Tall Wolf, what are you and other prominent Cherokees doing to solve the economic and social problems facing the tribe today? What are you doing about poor housing, unemployment, lack of adequate educational opportunities, and the disintegration of traditional Cherokee culture? Besides telling jokes, that is."

The lethal tightening of his facial muscles warned that she'd finally gone too far. Erica stared up at him stoically. The issues were too important to ignore.

He smiled, flashing white teeth at her in a predatory way that iced her blood. "I don't waste my time trying to answer complicated questions in a twenty-minute speech after dinner."

"Why? Do you feel that most whites really aren't interested in the plight of Indians today?"

He went very still, his bench-breaking hands clenched on the sides of the podium, his dark eyes holding hers with a look that made her knees weak. He seemed to be fighting some monumental decision. Whatever chord she'd touched, it was a deep one.

"Yes," he said softly.

She tilted her head. "Pardon me?"

He lifted his chin and said in a loud, firm voice, "*Yes.* I frankly don't think most of you give a damn."

That blunt remark sent a ripple of shock through the audience. Erica gazed breathlessly at James Tall Wolf, mesmerized by the challenge and the fury in his eyes, even though they were directed at her.

"Could you elaborate?" she asked.

"Hell, yes." And he did so nonstop for the next ten

minutes, his voice reaching through the ballroom like a dark whip. Erica sat down limply in her chair and watched him in awe. She sensed the crowd's electric response, and when she glanced at the faces around her she knew that whether they liked or disliked James Tall Wolf, they'd never forget him.

Neither would she.

He finished abruptly, shot her a cold look that brought her back to reality, and told the audience good night. He strode out of the ballroom without looking back, leaving a patchwork quilt of approval and disdain; areas of bright applause bordered by gray silence.

Erica barely heard the president's closing remarks. When everyone stood to leave she fumbled distractedly for her purse and briefcase. She felt empty, depressed; the night suddenly seemed bleak without the vibrant pull of James Tall Wolf's gaze. He disliked her, and she'd probably never see him again.

All right, she'd let him cool off for a few days, and then she'd get his phone number from the association's secretary and give him a call. She'd explain that she was part Cherokee and had only wanted to express a sincere interest in the tribe.

Getting wearily to her feet, she tucked her briefcase under one arm and endured silent frowns from the departing crowd. A few were not so silent.

"Thanks for insulting a guest speaker."

"Didn't know you were so interested in Indians."

"You broads never know when to shut your mouths."

To that remark she replied, "Blow it out your chimney, Harold."

She escaped to a rest room, where she gaped first at her ashen face, then at the disheveled state of her hair. Her dark blue skirt was twisted, and she'd forgotten to pull the jacket lapel over a small mud stain on her blouse.

Damn, she didn't care about her looks ordinarily; she'd never been able to compete with her mother or half sisters on that basis, so she'd stopped paying attention long ago.

"I love you," she told the chestnut-haired Amazon in the mirror, "but you must have looked homely as hell to the Wolfman."

The Wolfman. An appropriate nickname, even if he wasn't hairy.

The hotel hallway was deserted by the time she finished straightening herself up and headed for an elevator. Even the elevator was empty. Good.

Erica put her briefcase down, leaned gratefully against the cool, paneled wall of the elevator, and reached for the ground-floor button.

Her fingers bumped into a big, brawny hand the color of light copper. Erica jerked her hand back and gazed up into James Tall Wolf's dark eyes. Angry, watchful eyes.

It was true. Indians could track their prey silently.

He stepped into the elevator and hit the top-floor button. His intense, unwavering gaze never left hers as the door slid shut, closing them in together for a long ride up.

He planted both hands on the wall, trapping her between his arms. Erica gasped. He leaned forward, a muscle throbbing in his jaw, and said grimly, "I've been waiting for you."

# *Two*

---

"I wasn't trying to antagonize you."

"The hell you weren't." He leaned closer, his breath hot on her face.

Erica inhaled good cologne and a faint trace of rich cigar smoke; to her it was the essence of threatening masculinity. His hair was blue-black under the elevator lights, and his eyes were so dark that the pupils seemed to merge with their backgrounds.

"I don't need lectures from a knee-jerk liberal"—he spoke between gritted teeth—"who hasn't got one friggin' idea what it's like to be Indian."

"I have an imagination."

He whacked the wall by her head, and she jumped. "Then imagine this, doll. You're making a speech to a roomful of people. The last thing you need is a heckler. Most of the people in the audience already figure that because you're an Indian you're screwed up. You're a drunk, or on drugs, or you're lazy, or stupid, or you got where you are because of government handouts."

"You're wrong. A lot of people aren't narrow-minded."

"The other extreme can be just as bad." He bit each word off viciously. "They're hung up on the 'noble savage' stuff, and the last thing they want to hear is that we've got problems just like everyone else."

"I understand why you think the worst, but don't

misjudge *me*." Erica shivered slightly. Again she told herself that she knew how to deal with threatening men.

But not when she was alone with one of them in an elevator headed for the moon.

His deep-set eyes caught her tremor. They narrowed accusingly. "Are you afraid of me?"

*Yes* was not a smart answer, so she didn't say it. But it caught in her throat, and he saw it in her face. He cursed softly.

"I'd be afraid of you whether you were an Indian or not," she assured him. "I have equal-opportunity fear."

His tone was sardonic. "Injun no hurt paleface."

"Say that without growling and I might believe it."

"Dammit, what did you want from me tonight?"

She hugged herself and glanced at the passing floor numbers. "Nothing." They reached the top level and stopped. "Top floor," she quipped in a mechanical voice. "Sporting goods, appliances, amnesty for women with good intentions."

Without taking his eyes off her he reached over and hit the lobby button. She made a soft protesting sound as the elevator began to move downward.

"Women with good intentions," he echoed in a sarcastic tone. "Oh, hell, now I get it. The questions were just a come-on, a little bit more dignified than most. Congratulations. Your intentions got my attention."

Erica stared at him in astonishment. "No."

"Next time just shake that skinny behind at me instead. I'd give it a second look."

"You're mistaken. I'm not interested in jocks with egos bigger than their—"

"Oh, come off it."

His arms scooped around her, and he pressed her to the wall. Erica yelped just as his mouth sank onto hers with angry force, twisting, taking, proving a point. He stabbed his tongue between her lips and ran his hands over her rump, squeezing hard.

She stood on tiptoe, trying to escape, but her foot

slipped out of its blue pump and she lost her balance. Half-hanging off the floor with her fanny cupped in his hands, she squirmed against him and tried to shut her mouth.

He chuckled and reached one hand up to cup her jaw, the pressure not forcing her mouth to remain open but rather encouraging it not to close. He finally let go of her rump entirely, but that hand went straight to the front of her jacket, pushed the floppy blue material aside, and closed on one of her breasts with a gentleness that confused her.

Erica grabbed the lapels of his jacket, her hands fiercely twisting the material, but when his big, blunt-tipped fingers made her nipple swell even through a blouse and bra she didn't push him away. She simply held on for dear life.

Erica told herself that everything had happened so fast, she didn't have time to be rational. The fact that his touch was much more passionate than angry had a disastrous effect on her resistance.

"Hmmm," he said from deep in his throat.

"Hmmm," she responded hesitantly.

Then he willed her tongue into his mouth and attacked it as if it were a melting Popsicle.

Big Red Riding Hood was definitely about to be eaten by the wolf—and it amazed her that she didn't want to run away. Why? What was wrong with her? She was vibrating with blind, desperate excitement, and he knew it. Dammit, he knew it, and she was beyond caring that he knew.

Erica gave up and wound her arms around his shoulders. The shifting of her body brought her closer to him, and he flexed slightly, nudging her belly with a hard ridge.

James Tall Wolf pulled his mouth away from hers just enough to talk. "Your intentions are even better than I expected," he said hoarsely.

He frowned at her, his expression not so much angry as it was surprised. A painful realization cut into Erica. He hadn't expected her reaction or his own. He was shocked to find her desirable.

Wounded and embarrassed, she shoved him away. He stepped back tensely, watching her with a troubled awareness that made him look fierce. "Yeah, there's plenty under that blouse besides a bleeding heart." His voice was gruff.

She sagged against the wall, one shoe off, her blouse half out of her skirt, her mouth feeling so hot and swollen that she lifted a hand to it. "Touch me again and I'll kick an extra point right between your goal posts."

The elevator reached the ground floor, and the doors opened. A sweet-looking elderly couple stood there in the hotel lobby, holding hands. "Oh, my," the woman said pertly, peering in at Erica's disarray.

"Sorry. Excuse us." Erica pushed the button that closed the door. "No!"

But James Tall Wolf had already pushed the button for the top floor again. She gave him a lethal look. They were both breathing too fast. "If you wanted revenge, you got it."

He gazed down at her sternly, his arms crossed and his long legs braced apart. "A jackass at my table called you ugly. Are you?"

The question was so bizarre that she sputtered, "N-no!"

"Then get rid of that awful suit and buy something that fits. And pull your hair up so your face shows. And when men look at you, don't hang your head like some sort of wimpy old maid."

His words hit her in the solar plexus, but she drew her chin up and glared at him. "I don't know who you were looking at, but it wasn't me. You've got more money and power and reason for happiness than most people ever do, but all you can do is whine about being misunderstood because you're an Indian and then insult me with your stupid-jock notion that any woman who's nice to you wants to crawl into your bed."

She tucked in her shirt and quickly jammed her foot back in the lost pump. "I wanted to be your friend."

"So you stood up and made fun of me in front of people."

"I honestly didn't mean to." Her shoulders slumped. She was so addled at that moment that all she could think about was the feel of his mouth on hers and the damp heat he'd created between her thighs. She shook her head at him wearily. "Thanks for the education, Mr. Tall Wolf. You've taken care of any mistaken ideas I had about Indians. I guess I did think that you'd be more noble than the average sports-celebrity-turned-businessman. But you're just a spoiled jock."

He dismissed her with a fierce wave of one hand. "Fine. I'm not used to desperate, frumpy women who don't have the courage to ask outright for what they want."

*Frumpy.* Erica could stand most insults, but having this man make fun of her looks was too painful. "Take steroids again," she told him. "They couldn't make you any nastier than you are now."

His eyes flared. "Doll, if I were still on the macho juice you'd have gotten a lot more of your wishes fulfilled."

The elevator bumped to a stop. She grabbed her briefcase and started toward the door, not caring which floor they were on. He blocked her with one long arm. Erica nearly stumbled, trying to avoid contact with him.

"This is my floor," he told her in a low, challenging tone. "I don't think you want to get off here."

"No. I definitely don't."

He smiled wickedly. "Be honest. I might grant you a favor."

"I've never tried a one-night stand before, and I'd prefer to wait for a friendlier offer."

"You sound like you spend a lot of time waiting for *any* offer."

"And I doubt you have enough morals to turn down any offer. Good night, Rabid Wolf."

"She-Who-Makes-Noise, you're a hard woman to please." He chuckled harshly and walked away without looking back.

Goose bumps rose on her flesh. She felt Swift Arrow's obsidian eyes watching her as she washed her legs in the stream. Suddenly he moved toward her, his skinning knife in one hand.

Marybelle shrank back, frightened by the power in his muscular, half-naked body. He grabbed the neck of her gingham dress and gracefully slit the bodice to her waist.

"Indian women wear only a skirt. You are an Indian woman now, my woman. Those white clothes offend me."

Marybelle tried to cover her breasts with the halves of her slashed dress. His eyes began to burn with a primitive urgency as he studied her flushed skin.

"Don't fear, little one," he said with surprising gentleness. "I won't take you until you want me."

She gathered her courage. "Never. This slave won't love her master."

He grabbed her bodice and jerked it down her shoulders. "I will teach you different."

Marybelle gasped as he pushed her back on the soft grass and—

"Ricky, your mother's on the phone."

Erica fumbled with the book and dropped it, quickly kicked it under her desk, and snapped to attention. "Thanks, Marie. Got it. Right. Is my lunch here yet? Have you typed that contract to send to George Gibson? Where's my new box of floppy discs?"

Marie Stewart, never one to take employer-employee relationships seriously, frowned at her like a scolding nanny. "Are you all right?" The office manager glanced at an air-conditioner vent on a wall painted functional brown. "Too hot?"

"No. Why?"

"You're edgy, and you were fanning yourself a second ago."

"Too much coffee." *Too much James Tall Wolf,* Erica added silently. Too much thinking about the night before. Too much of that lust-in-the-teepee novel she'd bought on the way to work that morning.

"Your mother. Line two."

Erica slapped the phone to one ear. "Hello?"

Patricia Gallatin Monroe said what she always said when she called. "This is the Boston mother phoning her Washington runaway." In eight years the words had rarely varied. "I received your message."

"Hi. Your secretary said you were out of town. Something about catering a party for the Kennedys. Again?"

"Hmmm. They adore my people. I have the best pastry chef in Boston."

"Mother, I'm proud of you."

"I know. I did a marvelous job, as usual. Ask Lucianne. Your sister is still trying to steal my clients."

Erica sighed. Her mother's household ran on pride, propriety, and vigorous competition, even among family members. Erica's half sisters, Lucianne and Noelle, thrived on the system. It was either compete or get out. Erica had gotten out.

Erica the rebel. She looked down at her navy blue tailored dress. Little pieces of lint clung to it. Some rebel.

"I flew down to Georgia, day before yesterday, and met my Gallatin cousins."

There was dead silence on the Boston end of the phone. Finally her mother said, "I asked you not to."

"I'm going to study Dad's family. I want to know about them."

"Your father was white."

"One-eighth Cherokee."

"Why do you care, after all these years? You never cared before."

Erica rubbed her forehead wearily. "I never knew anything about the Gallatins because you refused to discuss them."

"You were so little when your father died in the accident. After I remarried I thought you wanted to feel like a Monroe."

"Not so little—seven years old. I never forgot Dad." That was an understatement. She still had all his Navy aviation insignia in her jewelry box.

Marie buzzed her on the intercom. "Boss, T.K. is on line one."

"Mother, I have to go. I just wanted you to know that my cousins are wonderful people. You'd like them. 'Bye."

Her head throbbing with tension, Erica punched the other line. "Are we on for tonight?"

A sinister, chuckling male voice came back. "The Nemesis Gang sallies forth again. Bring your hammer."


James stepped out of a cab on Sixteenth Street and gazed distractedly toward the White House, a few blocks away. The structure always looked majestic, sitting there at the end of one of the most important streets in the world—or at the beginning of it, if you were an optimist. James wasn't.

In the lunch crowd bustling along a tree-shaded sidewalk he caught a glimpse of shimmering reddish-brown hair, and his heart beat faster as he craned his head for a better look. She-Who-Makes-Noise?

He held his breath in anticipation until he realized that the redheaded woman was too short and stocky to be his redhead. His redhead. He looked away, grimacing. It was bad enough that he'd dreamed about her the night before, and that morning had considered calling the developers' association to get her name and phone number.

The last thing he needed was to tangle again with a cranky loner who liked to cause trouble. After a second he realized that he'd just described himself.

"Five bucks," the cab driver said impatiently.

James paid the driver quickly. "There you go."

"You Indian?"

"Yes."

"I've driven a lot of foreigners around, but you're my first Indian. That Gandhi fellow still in charge?"

James gazed at the driver solemnly. "Yeah. We reelected him head chief last month."

"Oh. That's nice."

James draped a rain slicker over one shoulder and jogged up the steps of a sleek granite office building. For a second he regretted wearing jeans and a white pullover among the sharply dressed office crowd eating lunch in the spring sunshine. He drew more than the usual number of curious gazes.

"Go, 'Skins," a young man yelled. "Hiya, Tall Wolf!"

James grinned and waved at the fan. Part of him liked the attention—he still got a kick out of signing autographs and talking to fans—but he also knew that their respect was tainted with morbid curiosity. They expected him to be outlandish and frightening.

He couldn't complain too much, because back in his playing days that was precisely what he'd taught them to expect.

Now he just wanted to be left in peace, and he wanted to go home to the graceful old mountains of North Carolina, where he wouldn't be so different, among his own people. That was where he'd go one day, that was where he'd stay, and that was where he'd find a woman who would help him forget about skinny redheads who made too much noise.

"We're goin' on a raid, my man," Stephen said in his thick Texas drawl as he tossed a basketball at a hoop on his expensively decorated office wall. Beside the hoop hung the annual *Sports Illustrated* swimsuit calendar. Stephen Murray, real-estate tycoon, good friend, and lady-killer, was the most laid-back businessman ever put in pinstripes.

James eyed his partner warily. "Like the time you left me in the girls' dorm with thirty pairs of panties stuffed under my shirt?"

"Hah. We're gonna trap us some carpenter ants of the human variety. And we're gonna put their carpenter-ant butts in the D.C. pokey."

James propped his feet on Stephen's custom-made teakwood desk and sipped a glass of brandy. "Does this have anything to do with the property downtown?"

"Our lovely block of vacant lot, yessir. I got me a tip from an inside source. Gonna have a carpenter-ant problem there tonight."

"Same kind as before?"

"Ants named Nemesis. Yessir."

James frowned into his glass. Nemesis was a coalition of architecture students who sneaked onto downtown property to build huts for homeless people. They had a slick game plan; in twenty minutes they could erect a cozy ten-by-ten hut complete with window and door.

The huts gave shelter and security to the saddest of the homeless cases—chronic outcasts who'd fallen through the cracks of the system—and Nemesis thumbed its collective nose at that system for being so heartless. He'd approved of the gang's tactics as long as it built huts on public property, but when the members grew bold about trespassing on private lots he lost sympathy.

"What's the deal tonight?" he asked.

Stephen chortled. "Gonna hide and wait, pal. Got me some private security boys lined up. I'm goin' along for the excitement. Thought you'd like to come too."

"What the hell. Sure."

James downed his brandy. What the hell. He had a limited amount of sympathy to go around, and he saved it for his own kind.


The first hut went up without incident. Twenty well-coordinated gang members, wearing dark clothes and ski masks, hammered and sawed, and christened the tiny dwelling with their victory cry, "Home, Sweet Home!"

Erica tugged at her hot, itchy mask and almost decided to pull it off—after all, Nemesis had been building huts for a year now without ever being caught. It was two A.M., and this part of D.C. wasn't exactly hopping with people.

But caution made her keep the mask in place, so she wiped sweaty palms on the legs of her overalls, rolled up the black sleeves of her work shirt, and helped hoist a prebuilt base into place for the second hut.

Suddenly the group was flooded by blinding light. "Do not move," a voice boomed over a speaker. "You are trespassing on and defacing private property. The police have been called. You are surrounded by security guards from Stephen B. Murray Developers. Do not move."

For a second there was tense stillness. Then T.K. yelled, "Plan B!"

Everyone dropped everything and scattered wildly. Erica raced into the darkness and dodged two uniformed guards of rather tubby proportions. Her heart threatened to knock a dent in her chest.

Erica Alice Gallatin, fugitive. Oh, Lord. First the incident with James Tall Wolf, and now this. Her staid self-image had undergone some bizarre changes in the past two days.

"Get the tall guy!" someone yelled. "He's heading for the street!"

Tall guy heading for the street? Erica faltered. They were after *her*.

She quickly recouped and ran faster, glad that she'd been a distance runner on the women's track team at Georgia Tech. The way adrenaline was pouring into her blood just then, she thought she'd come to a halt somewhere around Vermont.

She hit the two-lane street and aimed for an alley on the opposite side. If she were lucky it wouldn't be a dead end.

But then she heard feet on the pavement behind her, closing fast and taking long, forceful strides that made the patter of her own feet sound childish.

Frantic, Erica zipped into the alley, jumped a low pile of paint cans, and tripped on a soggy cardboard box. Who had they sent after her—the Incredible Hulk? The *thing* was right behind her, and suddenly it pounced.

She thought her back would break as two big hands grabbed her waist. Smashing into another stack of boxes, she fell on her stomach, with the thing on top of her.

Her breath exploded in a pained yelp. Erica imagined two popped balloons where her lungs had been; she figured her breasts looked like fried eggs.

She couldn't move; she couldn't inhale; she gasped like a beached fish as the thing rolled off of her and took her wrists in an iron grip.

The thing had a voice. "Sorry it had to be this way," it said, breathing with disgusting ease. "I didn't want to tackle you, but you've got a helluva stride. Get up on your knees, kid, and puke if you need to."

She managed to get her knees under her and crouched amidst the boxes, coughing. He—it—patted her shoulder. "Okay, kid?"

Erica nodded. The thing clamped a hand on the back of her overalls and helped her up. Her ski mask was askew, and she weakly tugged it back into place.

The thing snorted. "No need to keep the yarn face, kid."

He was laughing at her, and she suddenly realized that she had a lot more aggression in her Boston-bred soul than she'd realized. Erica lifted her head and croaked, "Kiss—"

The thing was James Tall Wolf.


She sat in a circle of her comrades, her arms locked with theirs, bathed in the lights of the television crews that had just arrived.

Erica's stomach felt like a knotted rope. Someone had not only squealed on Nemesis to Stephen Murray and associate—the victorious James Tall Wolf, who now stood on the perimeter, watching nonchalantly—but someone had also called the media. She suspected T.K., who was a known glory hound.

"Keep your masks on," T.K. called. "And go limp when they try to carry you off the lot! It's an old protest technique."

Erica peered out of her ski mask at Tall Wolf and was extremely glad that he didn't know whom he'd captured so easily. Anger tore at her. A man with his heritage ought to be sensitive to human suffering, yet he just stood there heartlessly, his expression shuttered.

She heard shouts of anger and jerked her head to the left. A tall, craggy-faced blond man in chinos and a sports shirt was moving along the circle of gang members, grinning merrily and pulling their masks off. He jauntily tossed each mask over his shoulder.

"Lookee here," he drawled. "Carpenter ants, Lord have mercy. Boys *and* girls. Right ugly bunch."

"Don't unlock your arms!" T.K. shouted. "Murray, you're an SOB."

"Been called that so much, I had it embossed on my checks."

Erica and her neighbors locked arms more tightly as Murray continued removing ski masks. She glared at James, whose troubled expression showed that he either had indigestion or didn't like what his partner was doing. Probably had indigestion.

"Whoo, here's a big ol' skinny ant," Murray said when he got to her.

The humiliation was too much for Erica. She was already a criminal, so she might as well go all the way, she decided. When Stephen Murray grabbed her ski mask, she kicked him in the shins with the hard-soled heels of her work boots.

"A fighter!" He grunted in pain and stumbled back, his mouth open in shock, her ski mask hanging in his hand. "A she-fighter!"

Erica glared up at him and shook her matted hair free. "Touch me again and I'll kick you so hard, your knees will bend in the opposite direction."

James ran over and halted by his injured partner. He stared down at her in astonishment. "You."

"You," she muttered back.

He dropped to his heels in front of her, his eyes riveted to her face. Erica felt the color rise in her cheeks as she gazed at him, resenting his easy power and the way the television lights shimmered around him like a silver aura.

He shook his head. "You wasted time and resources tonight."

"I guess all Indians aren't big on human rights," she replied grimly.

"Why didn't you stay on government property?"

"The homeless aren't just a government problem."

"You could have built the huts where they'd be left alone to do some good."

"We wanted to make a statement."

"An empty statement." He dismissed the subject with a wave of one hand. "Are you hurt?"

His concern caught her by surprise. "What?"

"Did I hurt you in the alley?"

"Ah. Yes!"

He rammed a hand through his hair. "Dammit, I thought Nemesis was a bunch of young college guys."

"No, we old alumni women take part too."

He gazed at her as if meeting her anew. "You don't look like the type."

She looked at him reproachfully. "*Frumpy* women, unite."

His expression hardened. "Be nice to me and I'll keep you out of jail."

"Forget it."

Police officers moved in then. James rose and stepped back, where Stephen Murray stood eyeing the group balefully, and her in particular.

"Have fun, y'all," Murray said in disgust. He turned

and limped past James toward a limousine waiting on the street. "You need a lift back to the hotel, Jim?"

"In a second."

Burly policemen grabbed Erica's neighbors and dragged them away from her. "Passive resistance," T.K. yelled. Erica kept her solemn gaze directly on James Tall Wolf's frowning face.

"Get up, ma'am," an officer told her. Erica glanced around. Members of Nemesis were being forced to their feet.

"No."

"Ma'am, if you don't get up voluntarily I'll have to make you get up."

"Go ahead."

Thick fingers dug into the pressure point on one side of her neck. Sharp pain zigzagged down her back, and she squeezed her eyes shut.

Erica couldn't help biting her lip when the officer twisted her arm behind her and pushed upward. "No," she said raspily.

"Get up, ma'am." He began pulling her up by her twisted arm. The pain made her back arch, but she refused to give in.

Two new hands latched under her armpits and lifted her to her feet. "Stop it," James said in a low, growling tone.

Startled, she stared up into his eyes. "This is my fight."

"I'll handle this, sir," the officer interjected tautly. "Walk, ma'am."

"Don't do it, Ricky!" T.K. called.

Erica cried out without meaning to when the officer pinched her neck harder.

"Let her go," James said abruptly.

She gazed at him in astonishment. "Mr. Tall Wolf—"

"She's in custody," the officer warned him. He twisted her arm. "Walk."

"You're hurting her. That's not necessary."

The officer was angry now. "Back off, sir." He called

over his shoulder, "Reece, gimme some help here!" Another officer trotted over. "Grab her legs."

Erica fumed helplessly as the two officers carried her to the van like a human hammock. She looked at James with a mixture of anger and gratitude. She wouldn't have been caught if it hadn't been for him and his superjock speed, but if anything could have made her cry just then, it would have been his unexpected concern.

And she was shocked when an officer pushed him but he refused to move. He stood with his fists clenched, his mouth a grim line, his dark eyes watching her until the door of the police van closed her away from his sight.

The media loved the colorful, combative Nemesis Gang. Local television stations gave big coverage to the arrests on their early-morning newscasts. Erica only heard about them because she didn't get up until nine. She'd left the D.C. jail at four A.M.

Gritty-eyed, she drove to a residential site to meet with her carpentry crew. Then she called the office to check for messages.

"Call George Gibson," Marie said in a troubled tone. "He's upset about the Nemesis thing."

Erica waited until she got back to the office. Then, her mouth dry, she phoned the developer, one of the most prestigious in the D.C. area. Ten minutes later she walked into the spartan room that served as Marie's office and the company's reception area.

Erica sat down and stared numbly at the floor. "He withdrew the contract."

Marie groaned sympathetically. "Oh, Ricky, no."

"I was supposed to sign it tomorrow. Five hundred thousand dollars' worth of business down the drain. Two houses in the best new development in D.C." Erica swallowed hard. "We would have grossed over a million dollars this year."

"We'll do it next year, boss."

"Gibson detests Nemesis. Of course, he didn't know I was a member until he saw the newspaper this morning."

"And your response was—"

"Sorry you feel that way, Georgie. Go hire a builder who'll let you run her private life."

"Oh, boss, I'm proud of you."

"Work's going to be kind of sparse around here for a month or two."

"Why don't you take a vacation? You haven't had one in years. You've got a good office manager and a good construction foreman. The jobs we're working on now don't need your supervision."

Erica leaned back in the chair and shut her eyes. Idly she fiddled with the gold medallion hanging around her neck. For some reason she'd felt compelled to put Dove Gallatin's gift on a chain and wear it that morning.

Gallatins. Cherokees. James Tall Wolf. If it hadn't been for him she would have escaped last night. It was his fault she'd lost half a million dollars that day.

He'd said she didn't know anything about being an Indian. Well, she'd learn, and she'd be a better Indian than he was.

Erica stood up, filled with grim resolve. "Marie, get me a plane ticket to North Carolina."

"What's in North Carolina?"

Erica lifted the medallion and looked at it thoughtfully. "My tribe."

# *Three*

He couldn't stand it any longer. He had to know who she was. So the morning after the Nemesis incident James called the developer's association and told the secretary he needed information on a member.

"Her first name's Ricky, she's tall, and she's got dark reddish-brown hair." James added silently, *She knows how to kiss and she knows how to fight.* He balanced a note pad on his knee and waited impatiently.

"Erica," the secretary told him. "Erica Gallatin."

James stabbed his pen into the paper. "Gallatin?"

"Of Gallatin Construction. The owner. Seven employees. Been in business for eight years. Specializes in residential."

She gave James the business address and phone. After he hung up, he sat staring at the information. Gallatin wasn't a name one saw often. It was a very odd coincidence that Erica and Dove had the same last name.

He groaned at his speculation. Coincidences happened, and there was no way a D.C. businesswoman with skin the color of apricots and milk could be related to a full-blooded Cherokee in North Carolina.

He phoned Gallatin Construction and got a pleasant but firm female voice.

"Ms. Gallatin is out of the office. May I take a message?"

"When do you expect her back?"

"She's out of town. May I take a message?"

"She'll be back tomorrow? Next week?"

"Are you from the television station? If you are, she has no comment."

Exasperated, James gave her his name. There was a long pause, then an icy "Leave your message. That's all I can tell you."

He relayed his hotel number. What else did he want to say? *Let's meet in the elevator again*? No. "That's all," he told the voice. "I'd like her to call me."

"I doubt she wants to talk, but I'll pass the message along. Good-bye."

He was suddenly listening to a dial tone. James cursed heartily and slammed down the phone. Where was She-Who-Makes-Noise? And how could he deal with this urge to track her down at all costs?

Erica hadn't had a clear-cut mental image of Dove Gallatin's house; she had even wondered if Dove had a house, because Dove's lawyer, T. Lucas Brown, hadn't mentioned a home or personal belongings in the will.

But here it was, perched halfway up a mountain in a little grove of oaks and maples, a small log-and-clapboard structure with a front porch so big that it looked like a jutting chin on an otherwise well-proportioned face.

She left her rental car under an enormous oak in the yard and walked around, eyeing the weedy ground for snakes. There was an old barn nearby, still in good condition; there was a concrete pad where a fuel-oil tank had once sat; there was an overgrown garden plot and a black mound, where decades of household trash had been burned.

The home's windows and doors were boarded over with new two-by-sixes; whoever had done the caretaking had wanted to make certain no one got inside. But the place looked solid enough to withstand almost anything; and that fact alone made her like it immediately.

Erica discovered a small back porch with a concrete well in one corner. The well was boarded over, but an old electric pump was still in place atop it. Charmed, she studied it with an engineer's interest in quaint gadgets.

Then she returned to the big front porch and stood gazing in awe at a panorama of rounded blue-green mountains so vibrant that a painter might have just finished giving them their spring coat. Delicate white clouds hugged the tops of the taller ones, and low in the valleys a late-afternoon fog was already gathering.

Erica shivered with delight. She understood now why these were called the Smokies: Mists shrouded them as if preserving ancient secrets. These mountains were older than the Rockies, more gentle in their grandeur, more hospitable. And the Cherokees had loved them for hundreds, maybe thousands, of years.

She squinted at a hawk gliding overhead and took a deep breath of air so clean, it made her feel fresh inside. Yes, she understood why people would fight to stay there. A friendly meowing sound caught her ear, and she looked down to find a fat calico cat walking toward her across the porch.

"Hello, kitty." She knelt to pat it. "Are you a Cherokee elf in a cat's body?"

The distant crunch of wheels on gravel made her look up anxiously. Dove's driveway was nearly a quarter-mile long; it occurred to Erica that she was effectively trapped at the end of it.

She stood, watching closely as a police car rounded the last bend, then sighed with relief as she noted that the car belonged to the tribal authorities. She studied the tall man who climbed out, and a puzzling sense of recognition tugged at her.

Dressed in neat slacks and a short-sleeved shirt bearing official emblems, he might have been an officer from any small-town police force, except that he was Indian.

Suddenly she understood. He looked like a slightly older, more solemn version of James, full of the same controlled power and easy self-confidence.

Nodding to her, he strolled to the foot of the porch steps and stopped. "Ma'am, you lookin' for someone in particular?" he asked in a gravelly drawl.

Erica smiled. "Word travels fast around here."

He nodded again. "I heard at the motel that you'd asked about this place. And the neighbors called when they saw you go up the driveway."

She puzzled over that. "What neighbors? I didn't see another driveway near here."

"Boy was on his way back from a fishing trip. Saw you from the woods."

Erica's spine tingled. The forest suddenly seemed alive with watchful eyes "I'm a relative of Dove Gallatin's. I just wanted to see her house. I thought I'd talk to the new owners, but I see that there aren't any."

"A relative of Dove's?" His voice showed his surprise.

Erica explained the family history, and as she did, his face took on a pleased expression. He really was a handsome man, and he reminded her more and more of James.

"So I've come down for about a week to learn about my Cherokee history," she said in conclusion. "And I'd like to know what became of Dove Gallatin's possessions —particularly anything that has to do with the family, such as diaries or a Bible."

The officer held out a hand. "Let me introduce myself. I'm the reservation's director of community services —fire, police, and sanitation. And I'm the U.S. deputy marshall around here. Name's Travis Tall Wolf."

Erica clenched his big paw so fiercely that he frowned at her in discomfort. "Do you have a brother named James?"

An odd wariness gleamed in his eyes. "Yes."

"I—well, I know him. We met a couple of days ago at a business dinner in Washington."

Travis Tall Wolf looked relieved. "Then he told you."

"Told me what?"

He stopped looking relieved. "About Dove."

"No." She paused, a sense of dread sinking in her stomach. "We were never really introduced. He doesn't know my name."

*We almost ravished each other in an elevator, he tackled me in an alley, but he doesn't know my name.*

"What about Dove?" she asked in an uneasy voice.

Travis looked at her grimly. "James owns her place. And everything she left in it."


James knew there was trouble the second he heard his brother's voice on the phone. For one thing, Travis never called; he left that social nicety to their sisters. He and Travis hadn't had anything pleasant to say to each other in years.

Travis didn't beat around the bush. "Erica Gallatin has moved into Dove's house," he told James. "I helped her pry the boards off the front door and I got the power hooked up for her."

"What?" James sat speechless and listened to his brother's explanation. When Travis finished, James had almost conquered disbelief. Erica Gallatin was related to Dove. But what in hell was she trying to do about it? "She can't stay in Dove's house."

"Then you come down and make her leave. It's her and her cousins' place by tradition."

"It's my place by law."

"You're a white man now, huh? Always call in the law to settle your personal problems? Or will you just try to solve your problems with money, like always?"

James bit back harsh words. He grieved for the days when he and Travis had been best friends, before tragedy sent them on different missions in life.

Travis had been his idol. Travis could have played college football and probably pro, too, but he'd joined the marines right of high school and had been sent immediately to Vietnam.

Three years later, when James turned eighteen, he'd been determined to join the marines too. Then Travis had come home with a piece of shrapnel buried permanently in one leg, and Travis had vowed to punch him silly if he didn't go to college and play football.

"Be somebody important and make us proud," Travis had told him. "You'll do more for your people that way than I ever did."

James had become somebody important and for a few years he'd made the family and his tribe proud. They'd never know the price he had paid to do that.

Now Travis spoke softly, fiercely. "The old man wants to see you. Becky and Echo want to see you." He paused. "So do I. I don't know if this Gallatin woman is sincere or not, but if she gets you back home, she's worth the trouble."

James gave a humorless chuckle. That was the problem—she *was* worth the trouble. "I'm on my way."

Erica left the motel in town and drove back to Dove's place early the next morning, armed with a crowbar, hand tools, and camping gear. She was in her element, wearing cut-off jeans, an old T-shirt, and ratty tennis shoes, her hair pulled up in a ponytail, and thick leather gloves covering her hands. She went to work on the boards barricading the windows, fueled by righteous anger.

How had James dared to buy this place out from under an old woman who needed money? How had he dared to try to put her in a nursing home against her will? The day before she was supposed to leave here, Dove Gallatin had walked into the woods, sat down under a tree, and died. Of grief, the staff at the motel said.

Erica wrenched another board free from its moorings and slammed it to the ground. Travis Tall Wolf hadn't told her the complete story, only that James had bought Dove's home and furnishings.

She walked around behind the house and began jamming the crowbar under the boards on a back window. She'd buy this place back. James Tall Wolf had a lot of explaining to do.

Erica flipped a set of Walkman earphones over her head, attached the tape player to the waistband of her cut-offs, and returned to work listening to the sound track from *Phantom of the Opera*.

The Phantom was singing his solo about revenge, when a hand grasped her arm.

Erica screamed and swung around with the crowbar raised in defense. James intercepted it with his free hand, jerked it out of her grip, and threw it into the weeds behind him.

"What do you think you're doing?" he shouted.

She gaped at him and stood there with her hand in midair. He looked tired and rumpled in loose khaki trousers and a wrinkled blue sport shirt; he must have traveled hard and fast to fly down this early and make the long drive from the nearest airport, at Asheville.

"I'm fixing up my family home," she said between gritted teeth. "I want to buy it from you."

His face was a mask of rigid control as he stared down at her through narrowed eyes that crinkled at the corners, not the least bit merrily.

Erica put the earphones around her neck and snapped off the tape player. The sounds of the spring day pushed eerily into the silence; katydids singing in the rhododendrons, birds chirping, her breath rasping like sandpaper on concrete.

"I said I want to buy this place."

"No."

"No one in town understands why you want it, Mr. Tall Wolf."

"That's none of their business."

"You took advantage of a woman who was almost ninety years old! My grandfather's cousin! I'm not sure what relationship that makes her to me, but Dove Gallatin was my family, just about the *only* family I have on the Gallatin side, and I intend to protect what was hers!"

During the tirade his gaze had gone to the thick gold medallion that lay near the center of her chest. He reached for it boldly, the backs of his fingers brushing across her breasts as he lifted the medallion for inspection.

Erica shivered with anger and frustration over the intimate way he always invaded her personal space. "That's none of *your* business," she told him, and took the medallion out of his hand.

She slipped it under the neck of her T-shirt and frowned at the way his eyes followed its journey.

"Where'd you get it?" he demanded.

"From Dove. And I want to know what it means. What did you do with her belongings? If she left any personal papers, I want them."

He smiled sardonically. "They wouldn't do you any good without an interpreter. Dove only wrote in Cherokee."

"There *are* papers, then. Where are they?"

"In storage."

"What did you do with her furniture?"

"I didn't do anything with it," he retorted. "Dove gave most of it away; what she left is in storage too."

Erica made a sharp gesture at the house and land. "Why would a man like you want a place like this? Did you con her out of—"

He cut her off with a hand lifted in warning and a look that could have started a fire. "I never conned her out of anything. We made an honest deal, and I paid her more than the place was worth. I plan to live here someday."

"You're kidding. Your brother said you haven't been home in four years. And not very often before that."

His voice never rose, but it became more commanding. "This land means something to me, more than it will ever mean to you."

"I'm not the only Gallatin who may want it." She told him about Tess and Kat. "Kat's practically full-blooded, and Tess is half. They look like Cherokees. You wouldn't deny them their heritage."

He turned away, shaking his head, his hands propped jauntily on his hips. "Sounds like they don't know any more about the tribe than you do."

"We can learn."

"It doesn't work that way. You have to live it. You have to grow up with it. You have to see the contrasts between the Indian and the white world."

"This is a heritage I'm proud of! Why do you want to keep me away from it? How am I hurting you?"

He swiveled toward her, his eyes glittering with anger. "You want to play at being an Indian. The glamour'll wear off as soon as you see that life's not quaint or easy here. You won't fit in."

*You won't fit in.* How many times she'd heard those words in her life. And they always hurt.

Erica went to the back porch and sank down on a step. She propped her arms on her knees and, blinking hard, tried to focus her anger on a solitary clump of grass between her feet.

"I've always been an outsider—in my mother's family after she remarried, in the construction business because I'm a woman, in social situations because I'm too tall, I'm too plain, I'm too aggressive. I don't expect to fit in."

She realized suddenly that she was trembling and near tears. It was mostly because James Tall Wolf's attitude disappointed her so much. He'd treated her with compassion several times in their brief acquaintance, but obviously compassion was not his trademark.

Erica stared harder at the grass clump and willed the tears away. "You think I'm not a Cherokee because I don't look like a Cherokee, but I can still want to be one, and nothing you do will make me stop wanting."

She glanced up as he came to the porch and sat on the step between her feet. Erica leaned back from the sudden closeness when he propped one hand beside her hip. He rested the other hand on his updrawn knee.

He'd lost a lot of his anger, for some reason she couldn't fathom.

"You're sincere," he said gruffly. "And don't ever think I don't admire that."

"Ah." She looked away from the searing scrutiny of his eyes, feeling awkward.

"But you're naïve. I've seen it before. It'll wear off quickly."

"What makes you so sure?"

"I've brought outsiders to visit the reservation. They never wanted to stay."

She propped her chin on one hand and tried to look casual. "Women, huh?"

"Yeah."

"Well, I'm not one of your lady friends, and you didn't bring me. I came on my own. So don't write me off so soon."

He looked unconvinced. "What do you think of the town?" he asked abruptly. "The truth."

Erica flinched inwardly, understanding his tactic. Cherokee, North Carolina, the largest town on the reservation, was a booming tourist trap that played up every Hollywood B-movie Indian stereotype ever created.

She shrugged. "I understand that the Cherokees draw more tourists than any other tribe in the country. The tribe makes a lot of money in the shops. And I heard about the bingo games. What incredible jackpots. The tribe must be making a fortune."

"Don't give me facts. Give me feelings," he urged softly.

It was impossible for her to resist the seductive plea in his voice. Erica looked at him wistfully. "Some of it's very sad. Cheap trinkets. Authentic Indian dance masks made in Taiwan." She nodded at the simple beauty around them. "I'm sure everywhere's not like that. I haven't had time to explore yet."

"It's not all like the town," he agreed, his voice husky. "I'm glad there are jobs and money coming in, but the tacky hype makes me crazy, especially since a lot of those businesses are owned by whites who get leases from the tribe."

"I heard that Dove Gallatin walked out into the woods and willed herself to die because she didn't want to go to a nursing home."

Slowly, he nodded. "She did. She had a way about her. The old people said she had powers."

"Did you . . . what part did you play in the nursing-home thing?"

He frowned. "What do you mean?"

Erica took a deep breath. "I heard that you had something to do with making her go."

His voice was bitter. "Like maybe I conned her out of her place so she had nowhere else?"

Erica nodded.

"Will you believe me or believe people in town?"

"I don't know. You're almost as much of a stranger as they are." She paused. "I want to believe you. I'll try."

He rubbed his forehead in mild exasperation. "I bought this place years ago because she needed money and she wouldn't take a gift. She had to pay back taxes on some piece of land she owned in Georgia, and she was desperate."

Erica wanted to cry. Gallatin land, in Gold Ridge. Oh, Dove. Oh, Wolfman. He'd saved the land from being sold for taxes. She owed him the truth about it. "It's mine now," she murmured sheepishly. "Mine and my cousins'. Dove left it to us."

James gazed at her with an expression of astonishment that quickly turned into a grim smile. "She gave up everything to save that land for you. Why don't you go stay there?"

"My cousins and I will reimburse you for the taxes."

"I bought this place. Dove paid the taxes."

"But—"

"This place is mine, and I'm not giving it to a bunch of five-dollar Indians."

"What?"

"People who get themselves on the tribal roll just to collect benefits."

Erica wanted to scream. "I feel like slapping you for that, but from what I've heard you'd slap me back."

He raised a finger and pointed at her with slow, furious emphasis. "When I was growing up my only goal in life was to be a famous football player, so that my people would be proud of me. I did what I had to do to make that happen.

"I did and said a lot of stupid, humiliating things when I was taking steroids, but I was willing to pay that price. Football's a tough game. I got punished and I punished back. But I never hurt anybody off the football field and I never hit a woman in my whole life."

She had watched his eyes as he talked, and the brutal honesty in them was obvious. Erica hung her head, embarrassed by her accusation. "I'm sorry I misjudged you."

When she looked up, his blank expression told her that her apology had surprised him. "When I'm wrong I say I'm wrong," she muttered.

His jaw was tight, his gaze thoughtful. A little disconcerted, he fiddled with a blade of grass at his feet. "I intended to let Dove live here as long as she wanted. But finally I did talk her into moving to the nursing home. She had arthritis so bad that she could barely walk. She was half blind. She couldn't stay up here alone any longer."

"But didn't she have family—"

James' expression went grim again. "Obviously not," he muttered, and rose to his feet.

Erica looked up at his ominous expression, the straight black brows pulled together, the clean-cut angles of his face looking majestic even in anger.

"If we had known," she murmured, "if Tess and Kat and I had known about Dove, we would have come to see her. We would have tried to help."

"But you didn't know because you never cared to find out. I don't really blame you for that. Just don't come up here now and try to take over. It's too late."

He headed toward the front of the house with a long, swinging stride, and Erica trotted after him. "I don't want to take over."

"You can't have the place," he said over his shoulder. "What were you going to do—stay here a week or so and then board it back up when you leave for Washington?"

He grabbed a hammer and a plank. "If you've got anything inside, go get it. I'm closing the place up again."

Erica stepped in front of him, fury scorching her skin, her hands clenched by her sides. "I'll go to the tribal council or the Bureau of Indian Affairs or wherever I have to go, and I'll get myself listed on the tribal roll."

He stared at her in dismay. "So you have checked out the system."

"Yeah, I guess that makes me a five-dollar Indian, all right. I found out that anyone who's at least one-sixteenth Cherokee can ask for land on the reservation. The council has to approve all transactions, and I'm going to ask it to take a second look at the way you bought Gallatin land. You're not very well liked around here, so I suspect I can at least get a hearing on my predicament."

"They may think I'm an arrogant bastard, but they won't like an outsider either."

"From what I've heard everyone worshiped Dove Gallatin, and they'll treat any of her relatives with respect."

His silent, frustrated glare told her she'd hit pay dirt. Erica thought about the half-million-dollar contract back in D.C., and smiled. She'd won a measure of revenge.

His voice vibrated with control. "What exactly do you want to do on your little vacation in Injun land?"

"Visit. Go into town and talk to people. Read books about the tribe."

"For how long?"

"I don't know. For once in my life, I'm not going to set a schedule." She eyed him regally. "What about those personal papers of Dove's? How can I get them?"

A dangerous gleam came into his eyes. A slow smile slid across his mouth. "There's only one way you'll ever get those."

Erica's regal confidence faltered. "How?"

"Never say 'How' to an Indian. Oh, excuse me, you *are* an Indian, I forgot. You'll have to prove it."

"How—I mean, in what way?"

He walked to the edge of the yard, his head down in thought, his hands shoved into his pants pockets. After a few seconds he turned around and said loudly, "You have to stay here for two months. At the end of two months I'll hand over all of Dove's papers, and I'll even find someone who reads Cherokee well enough to interpret them for you. And if you still want this place, I'll give it to you."

Erica leaned against a porch support and crossed her arms, not loosely, but with the hands clamped on the elbows to form a stubborn shield. Anyone who knew her well would have recognized the gesture as evidence of desperate inner turmoil. Thankfully, James Tall Wolf didn't know her well.

"Don't get upset," he called. "It's a simple offer."

She almost groaned. How could he be so stern and so insightful at the same time? "Two months? I have a business to run."

"If you could leave it to come down here, you must have a trustworthy foreman. I know the construction business. You don't have to stay on site if you've got a good straw boss."

Erica paced, her hands clasped behind her back. "Can I fly home for a day or two at a time, if I need to?"

He nodded. "All right, but you live here. This is home. And you'll learn what I tell you to learn."

She halted suddenly. "You're staying on the reservation?"

"For a while."

"You just want to make this difficult for me."

"Yeah."

Erica's shoulders slumped. "Do you disapprove of me that much?"

He didn't answer; he seemed to be struggling for something polite to say. "That's not the point. Because if you make it through two months here, you'll still go back to D.C. It won't matter how I feel about you."

*It matters to me,* she thought sadly. But she'd be sensible and accept the fact that he only thought of her as misguided and aggravating. Erica made a grim correction. When he felt the urge to prove his seduction skills in an elevator, he also thought of her as a lonely, willing old maid.

Well, there were no elevators here. There weren't even any buildings over two stories tall, from what she'd seen thus far, so she'd be safe, she thought drolly. Somehow, that didn't make her happy.

"I'll take you up on your deal," she called. "And I'll win."

He answered with a wolfish smile.


He left to visit his family but was gone for only an hour. When he came back Erica was vigorously pulling weeds from an herb bed along one side of the house. He roared into the yard in an ancient red pickup truck and slid to a stop, the truck's tires spewing sand.

Erica put her hands on her hips and huffed at his reckless driving, but didn't say anything. Even dark sunglasses couldn't hide the fierceness in his expression. What in the world had happened when he went to see his relatives?

He gunned the truck's engine and curled one long,

brawny arm out the window at her. "Get in," he called, with an impatient, come-hither gesture of his hand. "We're going on a tour."

"I'm busy." She pointed to the herb bed. "Weeding." She gestured at her sweaty, dirty clothes. "And I need to clean up."

"You need to do what I tell you to do."

"Lord, with an attitude like that it's no wonder no one down here likes you."

He gazed at her sternly for a moment, then wet his forefinger and made a mark in the air. "You scored a point, Red." He slung open the truck door, got out, and swept his arm in a ridiculously gallant gesture from her to the vehicle.

"Please, madam, do abandon your weeding and accompany me on a jaunt." He paused, eyeing her over the top of his glasses. "Wretched company though I am, I will try not to be a savage."

"Oh, I like savages," she quipped. There was something a little anguished about him, Erica felt, and that made her own stubbornness dissolve.

She tossed her gloves down and got in the truck through the driver's side. He vaulted in after her and slammed the door.

A second later Erica was hanging onto the dashboard with both hands as the truck bumped along the rutted driveway at about forty miles an hour. It was a relief when they reached the paved road and James could drive fast without jarring her insides.

"Where are we going?" she demanded.

"I want you to see how people live here!"

"Can't we do this later?"

"No! I'm in the mood right now!"

"Whose truck is this?"

"My grandfather's!" James gave a sharp, angry laugh. "Would you believe that two months ago I sent him the money for a new truck, and I found out today that he gave the damned money away?"

"Is he senile?"

"No, he just doesn't care about money!"

"What's wrong with that?"

She'd obviously touched a sore spot. James slapped one hand against the steering wheel. "What good is making money if you can't help your family with it? They're all so damned proud that they've never kept even half of what I've sent! They give the rest away! I considered it a big victory when one of my sisters agreed to take a new car from me for her birthday!"

"Well, they're obviously helping needy people here."

"Hell, yes, but I want to help *them*!"

"Sounds like you have. They take what they need and pass the rest along."

"What's the point of all I went through in nine years of pro ball if my own family thinks I'm a smartass whitey!"

"A what?" she asked in consternation.

"That's what Indians call a local boy when they think he's gotten too important for his own good!"

"Well, are you a smartass whitey?"

He gripped the steering wheel fiercely. "You can't shove a poor, ambitious kid from the reservation out into a big-league world and expect him not to be affected by it! Everybody in the whole damned tribe wanted me to go become a celebrity, but nobody wanted me to come back a celebrity!"

Erica covered her ears. "Roll up your window and stop shouting."

When he'd accomplished at least the first part of that request, he settled back on the seat and glanced at her apologetically. "You didn't want to hear me bellow about all that stuff," he said wearily. "I just get nuts when I come back to the reservation."

"Sssh." She patted his arm sympathetically. "Why in the world do you want to move back here for good one day, if that's the way you feel?"

"It's home." He gestured vaguely, trying to sum up deep feelings. "It sounds hokey, but there's something about being a Cherokee that makes these mountains part of my blood. I just have the feeling that I've always been meant to come back here, that this is where I belong."

"I understand that," she said wistfully. "When I find a place like that, I'm staying for good."

Abruptly he pointed out the front window. "Our tour," he reminded her. "I want you to see reality."

Erica gazed out at an old trailer set back off the road. The yard was weedy, and several nut-brown children played around a junked car. "The kids look healthy and happy," she noted.

"Uh-oh, I've got me an optimist."

"You need an optimist."

"Good. You've got the job."

He spent the next two hours driving her along tiny paved roads that wound through beautiful little valleys and hidden coves, then up mountainsides to breathtaking views of the forest. Along the way he made sure she didn't miss the rugged cabins, old trailers, and ramshackle farmhouses scattered among the woodlands.

Erica made sure he didn't miss a single nicely kept modern house, of which there were more than a few.

Finally she said, "I'm not shocked by poverty, James. I see a lot of pitiful situations working with Nemesis. This isn't pitiful, because there's plenty of happiness here. Sure, there are problems, but there're also big gardens and fat dogs and carefree children." She sighed. "Now, can I go back to Dove's place and clean up? I smell like an herb garden—dirt and all."

He swung the truck onto a narrow logging road. "Hang on, Red, I'm taking you to the bathtub."

Erica grabbed the dashboard and looked over at him anxiously. She didn't like the mischievous smile on his face.

"Bath time, native style," he announced, and drove off the road through the woods. A minute later the woods broke to reveal a beautiful mountain stream.

He began pulling off his blue sports shirt before he

cut the engine of the truck. "Shuck whatever you feel like shucking and hit the water," he told her.

Erica gaped at him and didn't budge. He got out of the truck, kicked off his loafers, and began unfastening his khaki trousers. "What are you shucking?" she asked.

He smiled at her smugly. "Red, you smell like a ton of catnip. Don't worry about me, just worry about being mauled by a purring bobcat. I hate catnip, and I won't bother you even if you go swimming with all your good intentions jiggling in the breeze."

"Thanks," she said dryly. There was nothing nicer than having a fantastically sexy man tell you that you smelled bad and couldn't arouse him even stark naked.

He dropped his pants, and she couldn't help glancing over long enough to see that he wore black briefs. That was the only look she gave his barely clothed body. A starving woman shouldn't look at filet mignon unless she expected it to be dinner.

With that interesting thought in mind she got out of the truck and marched to the stream, still clad in T-shirt, cut-offs, and tennis shoes.

"At least take off the shoes," James said as he trotted past her and splashed into the knee-deep water.

"I'm a-shucking." Divested of shoes she waded into the creek and sat down with her back to him. Now Erica understood how annoyed, aroused, and nervous she was—she was up to her shoulders in ice-cold water and it didn't even bother her.

"What the hell are you doing?" he asked, his voice full of laughter. "I mean, I know you're a city girl, but didn't anybody teach you how to skinny-dip?"

"Shut up, do whatever it is you came here to do, and leave me alone."

"I came here to play in the creek. It's hard to play when the person who's with you is impersonating a rock."

"You didn't indicate that you needed someone to play

with. Especially someone who smelled so bad that she might attract bobcats."

She heard sloshing sounds and realized too late that he was right behind her. He clamped one brawny hand on her shoulders, and she jumped, startled. To her surprise he merely patted her shoulder kindly.

"I didn't mean to hurt your feelings, or upset you," he said. "I just felt the need to go to water, and I thought it'd be a big joke to you."

She turned her head slightly and glimpsed a long stretch of taut male thigh. "Go to water?" Erica asked weakly and looked away.

"Clean the spirit. In the old days Cherokees were big on living near creeks and rivers. They loved the water. There were all sorts of purification rituals."

"Does it make you feel better?"

He chuckled wearily. "Something does. Maybe I just enjoy arguing with you. You don't take much bull."

She shivered violently, but a lot of it had to do with the situation. He thought she was grand fun; he didn't have the slightest interest in her as a woman, and it hurt. "I would really like to go back to the house now," she told him.

He patted her shoulder again. "Okay, Red, okay. I was just feeling reckless. It's been a bad day. Look, you stay here, and I'll go pull my clothes on. That way I won't embarrass you."

Oh, Lord, now he was talking to her as if she were somebody's maiden aunt. "I'm not embarrassed."

"Uh-huh. Just wait here."

Erica heard him leave the creek. A second later she was on her feet and striding after him. One discovery: He hadn't taken his briefs off. Another discovery: It didn't matter. He had the kind of fantastic derriere that provoked heart palpitations even when covered.

When he reached the truck and turned around he gazed at Erica in surprise. She nodded to him quaintly. "Nothing I haven't seen before."

Then she got in the truck and looked ahead without blinking until he got dressed.


No one had warned her that peace and quiet could be so unnerving. Erica sat on her sleeping bag in the middle of Dove's bedroom floor, a tuna-salad sandwich laying uneaten in her lap, her head tilted toward the window screen. Actually there were night sounds—the rustling of tree limbs, the poignant calls of whipporwills, a chorus of tree frogs.

But she'd been raised in cities, weaned on the unceasing hubbub that formed the background drone of urban life, and there in the mountains the night noises weren't sounds so much as a form of mysterious silence. They weren't human.

And the darkness beyond the window screen was deeper than any city darkness. She understood now why ancient peoples had created all sorts of myths about the night world.

Shivering, Erica squinted at the bare light bulb in an old fixture on the ceiling. More lights, that was what she needed. The next day she'd put up flood lamps outside. Just let the creepies try to get past a two-hundred-watt bulb.

She was exhausted from the long, grueling day. Cleaning house and pulling weeds had been easy, but the strange jaunt with James Tall Wolf had sapped her energy as a marathon race would. She ought to have been able to sleep. Erica got up and went to fetch the book she'd brought with her, the latest Stephen King novel.

She loved thrillers and suspense novels—they were such fun when read in the cozy confines of her condo bedroom. Suddenly she froze. On second thought, reading Stephen King might not be a good idea that night.

Something very real was growling outside the bedroom window.

·  ·  ·

James had borrowed his grandfather's truck, and the high-set headlights cast a bright arc of light on Dove's narrow, graveled driveway. They caught the two boys full in the eyes.

The pair, dressed in shorts and dark T-shirts, bolted into the woods that bordered the road. James cursed grimly and floored the accelerator. This was what he'd suspected.

Dove's house was dark, a mere outline against black woods. James leaped onto the porch and pounded on the door with his fist. Quick-running feet crossed the creaking porch as he whipped around, searching the darkness.

He heard an ominous whirring sound just as something sharp jabbed him in the arm. Pain and surprise made him react with automatic reflexes honed by years of competitive sports. He swung powerfully and cuffed the attacker with the heel of his hand. The boy was tall, and the blow hit him in the temple.

With a soft yelp the youngster crashed against the side of the house and slid into a heap at James's feet. The whirring sound stopped.

"Sorry, kid," James muttered anxiously, bending over. "But your game's pretty damned reckless." He latched his hands onto slender shoulders and felt his way up. Horror ran through him when his fingers curled into wavy, shoulder-length hair.

Oh, no. A tall kid. Not again.

She-Who-Makes-Noise was frighteningly silent.

# *Four*

Land of the Giants, that was what this was. Maybe she was just woozy from being thumped in the head, but for the first time in her life, Erica didn't feel too big.

She estimated that Echo Tall Wolf was six two and Becky Tall Wolf, the puny one of the family, was maybe five ten. Grandpa Sam Tall Wolf was nearly as tall as James, which meant about six five. Becky, Echo, and Grandpa Sam looked majestic even in terry-cloth robes.

Erica smiled groggily. Robes were the attire many tall people favored when forced out of bed at this time of night.

James kept one hand on her forearm and one between her shoulder blades as he guided her into a rustic den with a decor somewhere between a middle-class family room and a Cherokee museum. He sat Erica down on an overstuffed sofa and covered her in a colorful quilt as she squinted around at Indian paintings, woven rugs, a big stone fireplace, and lots of homey clutter.

"She needs some fresh ice," James said. He took the washcloth she held against her temple and dabbed her face with it.

Erica barely noticed the soreness radiating through the spot beside her right eye. No matter what she thought of James most of the time, that night he'd been utterly wonderful—except for knocking her in the head, of course, but she couldn't blame him for that.

She glanced at the angry bruise below the sleeve of his white golf shirt.

"I'm sorry I drilled you," she murmured again. "It was the only weapon I had."

"It's sort of funny. How many women are skilled in hand-to-drill combat?"

"I have to hear this story, but right now I'll get the ice," Becky Tall Wolf said in a soft, musical voice, and left the room.

"James, she needs to be checked by a doctor," Echo Tall Wolf scolded, trading a sympathetic gaze with Erica. Beautiful and majestic, with rump-length hair and a magnificent figure that had to be size sixteen at least, Echo knelt in front of Erica and held up a hand. "How many fingers?"

"Two. And three left over."

Grandpa Tall Wolf chortled. "She's all right."

Erica nodded, feeling uncomfortable under all the scrutiny. "James didn't knock me out. I just couldn't find my eyeballs for a minute."

James rubbed his own face with the washcloth. "I was more upset after it happened than she was."

Erica nodded, and patted his arm gently. "I haven't been carried so many places since I was in diapers. I hope he didn't get a hernia."

Becky came back with a cup of ice. Curvaceous, graceful, her ink-black hair cut in short, feathery layers, Becky looked like a modern earth mother.

Erica watched silently as James held the washcloth for Becky and Echo to arrange ice in it. "You guys make a great team. If first aid becomes an Olympic sport, you'll take the gold."

The woman laughed, and even James smiled. "If there were more of us, we'd start a basketball squad."

He wrapped the ice into a tight bundle. "Lie down, and I'll hold this in place for you."

Grandpa Sam tossed James a pillow from the recliner across the room. James put it next to his leg while Erica gingerly stretched out on her side. She put her head on the pillow and decided that an injured woman couldn't be called a flirt even though the top of her head was mashed cozily against a man's thigh.

So she enjoyed herself thoroughly each time his thick, ropey muscles flexed against her head. Who would have thought that a scalp could be an erogenous zone?

Gently James placed the ice pack on her temple and let his hand rest against her hair. "How's that, Red?"

"Fine." Fantastic. "This is the first time I've stretched out on a couch where my feet didn't hang off the end."

"James built this couch when he was in high school," Echo told her. "He did everything, even the upholstery."

"I build furniture. It's a hobby," James said with a touch of embarrassment.

*He's a builder, like me,* Erica thought happily.

"It was an anniversary gift to our parents," Becky noted.

"Where do your parents live now?"

"They were killed in a car accident a few years ago," James answered in a guarded tone. After a second he added, "Travis's wife and Echo's husband were killed in the same wreck."

Erica winced and raised her head. Echo and Becky sat on the floor, which was carpeted in well-worn deep shag, a pretty fawn color complementing their skin tone. Grandpa Sam sat in the recliner, an unlit pipe in his big, gnarled hands. He had luxurious white hair that hung below his shoulders, and his weathered, craggy face made Erica think of a nice old walnut tree.

His and his granddaughters' expressions were somber, touched by memories that would always be with them.

"I'm sorry about your loss," Erica said softly. She couldn't turn her head to see James, but she felt his fingers brush her cheek in gratitude.

"Be still. Let your brain settle."

She rested her head on the pillow again. "Does Travis live near here?"

"He has a trailer in the woods a few miles off," Becky said. "He's building a house beside it."

"Ummmph," Grandpa Sam offered with disdain. "Some year."

He added more comments in a long string of undecipherable sounds, although he kept repeating Travis's name in a way that said Travis was a source of concern in the family. Erica tingled with excitement as she realized Grandpa Sam was speaking Cherokee.

James answered him in the same language. It was the most intriguing thing Erica had ever heard, full of long vowels and round tones, with emphatic pauses. It came from the back of the throat, and the few consonants she noticed were only languid hints of their English counterparts.

When he finished everyone was silent for a moment, and she sensed old disagreements in the air, "No more," James said.

"We're not trying to shut you out, Erica," Echo added quickly. "We don't usually speak Cherokee in front of guests. I apologize."

Erica waved a hand excitedly. "I love the language. I want to learn it. Would it be difficult?"

"Try this," James offered. *"Gah yo, le sa lon Cha-lag-gee."*

*"Gah yo, le sa lon Cha-lag-gee."*

"There. You said, 'I speak Cherokee a little.' "

She repeated the sentence several times, smiling.

"Good," Becky told her. "Now you're fluent in one sentence. The rest is easy. Now say, *Do yu nay ga je nah we.*"

Erica dutifully repeated the words. "What's that?"

"I am of white origin."

"Ah. No. My great-great-grandmother was Cherokee. Katherine Gallatin."

"Don't argue with this woman," James warned his sister. "She packs a mean drill."

That sparked new curiosity. Nothing would satisfy James's family until he recounted the night's lunacy in detail. Then they wanted to know about Erica's Cherokee history, and why she'd decided to visit the reservation. She carefully omitted any mention of her bargain with James.

"James can bring you to the museum tomorrow if you want to buy some books about the tribe," Echo told her. "I teach elementary school, but during the summer I work at the museum store. I'll pick out some good texts for you."

"And when I have time I'll take you to rent some furniture for Dove's house," Becky added. "I run a restaurant on the tourist strip, but I've got a couple of free hours after the lunch rush."

Erica tried to smile her thanks at the Tall Wolf sisters, but couldn't move her head enough without disturbing James's touch. She wanted to lie there forever, her head against his leg, feeling his hand gently rub the ice pack over her temple. The thick, callused pad of his thumb kept brushing her cheekbone.

Of course he was just being polite because he felt guilty for whacking her, but she wouldn't quibble over that. She nudged his leg. "Do you really think that those boys didn't mean any harm?"

"No, not the way they were running from a drill-carrying mountain witch. They weren't exactly tough punks."

"Aw, of course not," Sam added.

"Dove's house is supposed to be haunted," James explained. "Going up there to pester you was an act of courage."

"Uhmmm. Like counting coup in battle?"

"I don't know if Cherokees ever did much coup counting," James answered wryly. "We didn't fight very often after about 1800—not against the whites, at any rate. We did help Andrew Jackson beat the Creek Indians during the War of 1812."

"And see how little good it did us?" Sam said in consternation, as if he'd been there. "Jackson got elected President, and he kicked us off our land! We shoulda helped blast him."

Erica's thoughts were still tuned to her unwelcome visitors. "Did those boys want to scare me because I'm white?"

"Could be," James murmured. "Most of the tribe are mixed-bloods. They're friendlier to tourist types than the full-bloods, as a rule. There's a conservative element that doesn't want much to do with the outside world. Dove's house is in a conservative community."

*Tourist type.* Erica was disappointed James had classified her that way, even though his arrogance shouldn't have surprised her. She phrased her words carefully. "Does the Tall Wolf family fit the conservative description?"

"Moderate," Becky answered. "We want to preserve the old ways and benefit from the new."

"We welcome anybody who wants to fit in," Echo assured her.

Erica smiled. Take that, James. "I'm glad."

"We'll see," he announced grimly. "Time for bed." He got up and held out a hand. "Come on. I'll put you in my old room. The gals and I'll take turns checking on you to make sure you're all right."

"I'm fine," she insisted. She tried to take his hand, but found herself being hoisted into his arms again. He made the effort so nonchalantly that she felt almost little. It was a wonderful discovery.

"Good night. And thank you," she told the others hurriedly as James carried her out of the room. They looked a little shocked by his actions, and she wondered if he'd done something that was unusual for him.

He climbed a short set of stairs and moved sideways down the second-story hall so that her feet wouldn't bump Indian artifacts and family portraits on the wall. Erica glanced around curiously. Seams showed on the pale green wallpaper, and the carpet had a foot trail in the center, but the ambiance was homey rather than shabby.

"Good floors. Solid construction. Careful attention to detail," she observed.

"Thank you, carpenter ant."

She almost grinned at him. "The spirit is friendly. Where I grew up in Boston, the housekeeper yelled at us all the time."

"My mother never yelled. She just roped off rooms and threatened to set them on fire if we didn't clean up. My father called it slash-and-burn housekeeping. But it worked. When I got my first pro contract I gave them the money to build a new house, but they wanted to keep this one."

He carried her into a small room crammed with storage boxes. James worked his way along a cleared path to a bed that was twin-sized in width but giant-sized in length. "You made this bed frame," she said matter-of-factly.

"Yep. The mattress isn't as long as the frame, so the end is stuffed with pillows."

He put her down on a thin red blanket with a geometric eagle design woven into it. Erica glanced around at walls covered with high-school and college football memorabilia. He cleared his throat awkwardly.

"My parents kept it like a shrine."

"They must have been proud."

"Yeah. There were a lot of things I wanted to give them in return, if they'd lived."

She looked at him in quiet sympathy. He frowned, and gestured toward the long, slender legs sticking out of her cut-offs. "Get rid of those."

Erica chuckled nervously. "My legs?"

"Those shorts. Wear jeans or skirts. You don't want to look like a show-off. The old folks will approve of you quicker if you're a little on the prim side."

"No one has ever accused me of flaunting these knobby knees. And I've always been on the prim side."

"Not in those shorts," he insisted.

She stared at him in bewilderment, and finally decided that her legs were such bean poles that the sight bothered him. "James, in town I saw plenty of homely tourists in short-shorts and halter tops. If nobody is offended by them, they won't give a second glance to my legs in respectable cut-offs."

"If you want to be a tourist, go ahead," he retorted, his face stern. "If you want to get your hands on Dove's papers, do what I tell you to do."

Her friendly thoughts about him faded in a burst of aggravation. He was not only insensitive for hinting that her legs were ugly, he was also manipulative and stubborn. "All right," she muttered.

Her temple throbbed, and she cupped her hand over it. He looked at her closely.

"I'll bring you some aspirin."

"I'm fine. And no one needs to check on me during the night."

"Look, I was knocked out once during a playoff game. I went to bed seeing ten toes and woke up seeing twenty."

"I hope you told that woman you had a good time, even if you couldn't remember it. Happen often?"

Exasperation glittered in his eyes. "All the time." He turned and stalked out of the room.

Five minutes later Becky brought water and aspirin. "James sent me. He's bedding down on the couch."

Erica smiled grimly. And counting his toes, no doubt.


She was building a bridge, and the work was darned hard, considering that she was doing it from bed. Erica saw James smiling at her across a deep mountain gorge. His big, bronzed body was covered in nothing but a loincloth.

That alone made her work faster.

She couldn't move her arms and legs very well. She looked down and found herself wrapped in wide pieces of elastic material, stark white material that wanted to hold her like a spider's web.

But nothing could stop her determination to build a bridge to James, and she struggled fiercely against the bonds.

"Red, calm down. It's only a dream."

How had he crossed that gorge without a bridge?

Erica lurched upright, struggling against the elastic, then blinked awake and realized that James had a gentle grip on both of her wrists. The bedroom was shadowy; the door stood open, letting in a shaft of light from a hall lamp.

James sat on the edge of the bed, wearing only his jeans, one leg drawn up by her hips as casually as though she and he were old pals. She gazed blankly at an expanse of broad, well-developed chest, then at big shoulders defined with fluid muscles and the outline of veins that she could have traced like rivers on a map. The warm, musky scent of his exposed skin triggered a desire to nuzzle him.

"You looked like you were hammering in your sleep," he said wryly.

"Mmmm." She figured that now she looked like a large owl staring at him in the dark. "I was building. I'm a builder. Like to build things. Make them last, build them strong."

"I get the point. I'll let you go back to work in a second. This is your four A.M. brain check."

He put her hands down on his denimed knee and carefully slipped his fingers into her hair. He pushed it back from her forehead, turned her face toward the hall light, and gazed at her temple.

"See any holes?" she asked.

"Nope. You hide them well." He cupped her chin and looked into her eyes. "A little test. Full name?"

"Erica Alice Gallatin."

"Alice?"

She huffed. "What's your middle name?"

"Grange. After Red Grange."

"What's a Red Grange?"

"You *are* brain-damaged. Red Grange is an immortal. He played football for the Bears."

"A Wolf named after a Bear. Makes sense." With James's big, callused fingertips touching her, not much else made sense right now.

He lifted her chin a bit. "Age?"

"Thirty-three."

"Hmmm, could be a few years younger. I'll have to take your word for it."

"Thank you, Dr. Kildare. You finally said something complimentary. And how old are you?"

"Thirty-six."

"Ah. A few good miles left in the old crank."

"Everything still works."

"You do a lot of road tests?"

"Depends on who starts my ignition." He cleared his throat and frowned at her. "Back to your test. Name your last two lovers."

Erica eyed him askance. His banter did dangerous, delicious things to her. For one, it transformed her cotton T-shirt into an erotic covering that scrubbed her breasts and made them tingle.

"None of your business."

"She-Who-Makes-Noise and None-Of-Your-Business. An interesting couple, sounds like. And the second boyfriend?"

"Name your last twenty lovers," she countered.

"Hmmm. I left my weekly appointment book downstairs. I'll have to check."

Erica casually pulled away from him. "You must be exhausted from carrying that ego around. Good night."

"One more test." He held up his hand and asked in a coy, singsong voice, "How many claws is the monster showing?"

"Three. Four if I count the extra mutant thumb."

He chuckled in a low, taunting way. "Go back to sleep and build an outhouse for your attitude."

James chucked her lightly under the chin, then got up and ambled toward the door, his thumbs hooked in his jeans so that the waistband rode low around his hips. Erica watched light gleam sensually on his taut skin.

"I'm a glutton for punishment. Tell me, Wolfman, what do you dream about?"

He turned around, filling the doorway. The hall light silhouetted him in heart-stopping detail. With a slow, languid movement he raised one hand and pantomimed throwing a football.

"Playing," he said softly. "You're a builder. I'm a player. And I play to win, Red. Fair warning."

Speechless, Erica watched him stroll away.

James had left to go fishing with Travis the next morning by the time she got up, but he'd set her suitcase in the bedroom and taped a note to the handle.

"No cut-offs."

She tore the note in half and left it on the pillow when she made his bed.

Erica ate breakfast with Echo, Becky, and Sam in a big country kitchen decorated in a style Sam called "Discount Store Deluxe." The food was great, the company congenial, and four big, goofy hound dogs lay under the table, politely accepting tidbits of food.

Erica was charmed, but a hundred troublesome questions tugged at her. Many of them she couldn't ask—at least not this soon, because they were too personal.

What had caused the rift between James and the family? It was obvious that the Tall Wolfs were all glad to see one another, but the tension remained.

She mentioned what James had said about moving back to the reservation and living in Dove's house someday. Echo, who at only twenty-nine was ancient and cynical compared to twenty-five-year-old Becky, made a disparaging sound in her throat.

"Maybe when he's through playing in the outside world. He says he won't settle down until he gets old and rich. Then he's going to move back here and get married. Dove's house will fall down before that happens."

Erica idly shoved a spoon back and forth in her coffee. "So he's saving himself for some sweet young thing he'll find on the reservation?"

Becky smiled puckishly. "Saving? More like he's collecting dividends until the right woman closes the account."

Erica forced a smile in response. "Lots of dividends, I imagine."

Grandpa Sam was reading a copy of the tribal newspaper. He rattled it for attention and said, " 'Spect he's gonna visit some dividends while he's here."

"Maybe not," Echo said cheerfully, and smiled at Erica.

Erica shrugged, and prayed James's sisters wouldn't suspect that she had a crush on him. A crush? Hopeless. She thought of romance in high-school terms—no, junior-high-school terms. James would be grandly amused if he ever found out.

"Nobody really knows what James will do next," Becky added quickly. "He's changed a lot in the last few years."

"Oh? Why is that?"

Echo spoke as she began clearing the table. "After the wreck. He'd been playing football for a lot of years, living in Washington, and people here said he thought he was too good to come home anymore. That wasn't true. He was just busy. He visited when he could, and he sent money and presents you wouldn't believe."

Becky picked up the story. "When the accident happened, James came home right away, of course. There were some problems with the case, because the tribal police didn't handle the evidence right. Travis wasn't in charge then."

"Problems?" Erica asked.

Becky nodded. "See, the accident was caused by a drunk driver—the wife of a sheriff from one of the counties around here. The reservation police had stopped her for drunk driving a few hours before she ran into . . . into our folks' car. But because she was important, and maybe because she was white, as James claimed, they let her go."

Sam put his paper down. He folded it with extreme care, his knotty fingers trembling a little. "James meant well," he said huskily. "He wanted to bring in a bunch of Washington lawyers to fight in court. He wanted to see justice done for his family."

"But we thought it ought to be kept local," Echo explained. She wound a dishcloth around her hands as she stared out a window at sunrise on the mountains. "We like to handle our own problems as much as we can."

Sam patted the pocket of an old sports shirt, then looked down, frowning, at his gray sweat pants. "Can't find my pipe," he muttered.

Echo said something gentle in Cherokee and handed him the pipe from an ashtray beside his newspaper. Sam fiddled with it as if the feel of the smooth gray surface was comforting. "Soapstone," he told Erica, holding up the pipe, his hand trembling more than ever. "Hand carved. This is what almost everybody used back in the old days."

Erica swallowed hard and tried not to embarrass him by getting teary.

Becky touched her arm, and when Erica swiveled to look at her, she murmured, "So Travis and the rest of us wouldn't let James bring in his lawyers. Things didn't go so well, and the woman, well, she was let off without much of a penalty."

Echo turned from the window, her shoulders slumped. "James has never gotten over that. He blames Travis, mostly, because Travis was the one who felt the strongest about handling the case ourselves."

Erica touched the sore spot on her temple, which throbbed anew from all the information she'd absorbed and the confusion it had created in her mind. She understood a few things much better now. Although James hadn't always been popular over the years, his family had known that his motivations were the best.

"The whole tribe put James under a lot of pressure," Becky said, as if reading her mind. "When he went off to play football he knew he couldn't let anybody down. And he didn't. He was a great football player. But that kind of success comes at a price."

Erica nodded. "You know," she said softly, "I've never heard a more eloquent speech than the one he gave about the Cherokees the other night in Washington."

"What speech?" Becky asked.

Erica looked at everyone askance, then explained. They were astonished.

"We never knew that James gave speeches defending the tribe," Echo said.

Erica nodded. "Yes."

Their eyes gleamed with pleasure, and they said a few words to one another in soft, rapid Cherokee. Erica felt she was building more bridges that morning, and when she saw the smile on Grandpa Sam's face, she knew the bridges would last.

By the end of the day Erica had furniture—funky, lime-green furniture rented from Trader Tom's Motor Lodge, but she didn't mind. Because Dove's two bedrooms were tiny, Erica put the queen-sized bed and the dresser in the living room, along with a couch covered in green vinyl. She decided wryly that the arrangement looked like a low-rent bordello.

The kitchen now sported a table and four green chairs, plus mix-matched dishes and cookware loaned by the Tall Wolf sisters. The old cupboards were stocked, and a small bookcase in the living room/bedroom held a dozen texts Erica had purchased at the reservation museum.

It was home—at least for now—and she felt content. After she ate dinner Erica donned her cut-offs over a black bathing suit and watched the sunset from a rocking chair also loaned by the Tall Wolf household.

That night she lay in bed reading *Myths and Sacred Formulas of the Cherokess* by the light of a lamp on a lime-green nightstand. There were formulas for everything from doctoring to romance.

Erica found one called "To Fix The Affections" and smiled thoughtfully. Well, what the heck.

"Now the souls have met, never to part. His eyes have come to fasten themselves on one alone. Whither can his soul escape? Let him be sorrowing as he goes along, and not for one night alone."

Erica paused. Good. Perpetual sorrowing on her behalf. "Let him become an aimless wanderer, whose trail may never be followed."

Take *that*, James, she added.

She suddenly felt very free from worry, and in celebration she stripped naked. Erica stretched out on top of the blanket, loving the brisk spring air on her body. She turned out the light and began to doze, lulled by the big new flood lamps she'd installed on each corner of the house. Through an open window she heard the forest moving in the night wind, the trees whispering secrets she badly wanted to learn.

Her last thoughts before sleep were happy. *An aimless wanderer . . . sorrowing as he goes along.*

The next thing she heard was the click of the lamp and a low, masculine groan of dismay.

# Five

James thought later that it was like finding an unexpected gift without the gift wrapping.

In the second before Erica gasped and scrambled to the other side of the bed, pulling the blanket up to her chest, he glimpsed a long, svelte torso with beautiful breasts and a taut stomach just made for a man's lips.

He groaned because that kind of temptation was the last thing he needed. Seeing her in shorts and a T-shirt the day before had convinced James that "skinny" was a description he'd never use again. She was a tall, coltish woman, but her angles were soft, and his senses went into high gear whenever he imagined how her body would feel under his.

"What are you trying to do?" she yelled, her eyes like green ice. "Do you want to be drilled in a spot that really hurts?"

No. Particularly not at the moment, he thought.

James sighed and backed away from the bed, his hands up. "I knocked. You didn't wake up. I have a key to the front door. I didn't expect you to be in the living room naked."

"What are you doing here?"

He nodded grimly toward a heavy leather tote bag on the floor. Then he caught her gaze and held it. "Moving in."

Her eyes widened, and she looked like a wild mare about to paw the ground. Lord, he'd liked to have been the man who gentled her to ride.

"Why do you want to stay here?" she demanded.

"One, I own the place. Two, there's an extra bedroom." He looked around drolly. "Two extra bedrooms, apparently. Three, I hate motels."

"You have a bedroom with nifty football pennants on the wall and a rock collection glued to the windowsill. Yes, I lifted the curtain and noticed. Why don't you stay with your rocks?"

James wasn't about to explain how much it hurt to visit a home filled with photographs of his parents, Echo's husband, and Travis's wife. He wasn't going to explain that he wanted to cry when he overheard Grandpa Sam solemnly reading the newspaper aloud to them, so they wouldn't miss out on tribal happenings.

And he wasn't going to tell her that the day's fishing trip with Travis had been a bitter fiasco of grief and anger that had ended with Travis telling him quietly that they were no longer brothers.

"I'm moving in," he repeated fiercely. "I won't bother you, so don't sit there like a spinster-on-the-half-shell, looking as if you're afraid I might take a bite."

He tracked the rise of fury in her fair complexion. With her face flushed and her hair tangled like a chestnut mane she looked not only wild, but violent.

"I'm not afraid. I know what to do and how to do it right," she said in a seething tone. "I know where to put what and what happens if I put it there."

"Now if you could only get somebody to put it there for you."

She twisted the blanket in one fist and pounded the bed with the other, all control gone. "I was married for eight years! It's not my fault that I'm a virgin!"

They stared at each other in shock, she looking as surprised as he felt. Then her head drooped, and she covered her face with one hand.

"I'm joking. What a dumb joke. You didn't even smile."

"You're not joking. Too late for a recall."

James looked for a place to sit down. All this time when he'd teased her about her attitudes he'd never dreamed she was a virgin. He'd never encountered a virgin before, much less one over thirty.

He went to the ugliest green couch he'd ever seen, sat on the edge of a cushion, and waited until Erica lifted a troubled gaze to his.

He watched her shiver visibly.

"I should have gone into journalism." She moaned. "I know how to broadcast news without thinking first. Congratulations. You're the only stranger I've ever told my sexual history to."

"Well, Erica Alice," he said numbly. "Well."

She shook her head in defeat. "When I tell people I'm an old maid, they believe I'm kidding. I'm not. There. Think what you want."

"Doll, you've gotta explain how you could be married for eight years and still qualify for volcano sacrifices."

"Catch my story on *Oprah Winfrey* next week. The 'Oddities of Nature' show."

"Look, we're going to be housemates. I'm not a stranger. And I'm great at keeping secrets."

"We're not going to live in this house together. If this community is so traditional and conservative, what will people say?"

He arched one brow. "Relax. If they say anything at all, they'll blame the big bad wolf for corrupting you. You'll get sympathy."

"Why didn't you tell me up front that you intended to stay here?"

James pretended to study his watch. "Can we discuss this tomorrow? I can't wait to get a good night's sleep on this comfortable couch."

Her voice was ragged. "This is just another way to antagonize me into leaving. Dammit, you're really cruel."

James stood ominously. "If I were cruel I'd lock your butt out of my house and say to hell with the consequences."

"You wouldn't like the consequences, I promise."

The day's frustration and fatigue boiled over. James strode to the bed, snatched the blanket with both hands, and jerked it away from her. She backed off the bed like a cornered animal, hugging her arms over her breasts.

"Out," he commanded, and pointed toward the front door. He figured he'd let her sit on the porch for five minutes, then toss her the blanket and apologize.

She gaped at him as if he'd lost his mind. "*No!*"

"You want me to carry you out?"

She heard the determination in his voice and edged warily toward the short hallway that went to the kitchen and bedrooms. "Let me get my things," she said between gritted teeth. "And I'll go to a motel."

"No." He waved a hand at her nakedness. You want to be a native, then go outside like a native."

"You're despicable!"

He smiled with malevolent pleasure. "I don't use my seat belt, I drop cigar ashes in houseplants, and I thought *E.T.* was a so-so movie." He pointed. "Out."

She had nothing left but dignity, and she used it. His heart twisted with admiration and self-rebuke as she straightened imperiously, lowered her arms, and walked past him to the door.

He caught the unadorned, squeaky-clean scent of her hair and skin. He saw the pride outlined in every inch of her backbone, though muscles quivered around it. She had to know that he was looking at everything below her backbone, too, but he suspected that she didn't know how perfect that part of her was.

She didn't have much padding, but it had found the right places.

Without looking back she slung the door open. James cursed under his breath. "Forget it," he said gruffly. "It was a dumb joke. I'm entitled to one myself."

She paused for a moment, glanced over her shoulder, and said with icy disdain, "I'm going to prove something to you. I may be an old maid, but I'm a hell of a tough old maid, and I don't need your patronage."

Then she stepped onto the porch and slammed the door behind her.

James followed her to the porch. She descended the steps and walked across the yard, looking incredibly majestic even in the harsh lights of the flood lamps. His mouth opened in dismay. How the hell could a man deal with a woman like her?

James watched in disbelief as she strolled into the darkness. "You'll get bitten by gnats, and the nights are cool up here even in the summertime," he called.

"Cold gnats are preferable to staying in the same house with you," she called back.

Then he heard only the silence of the night; it had captured her, taking her away for who knew what purposes. He'd either have to go after her and drag her back, strip naked and go sit with her, or let her suffer nobly.

He didn't think she'd appreciate any of the options.

James paced the porch, unwillingly thinking about *Utluhtu*, the spear-fingered monster who haunted the forests, stealing people's livers; and *Uktena*, a giant, dragonlike creature so dangerous that just looking at it could be fatal.

He chuckled harshly. And those two were just the tip of the arrow, where Cherokee monsters and evil spirits were concerned. No matter how modern and questioning and cynical he became, a part of him would never forget the stories he'd learned as a boy.

And Erica was out there thinking gnats would be her worst problem.

When he heard her scream he flung himself off the porch and hit the yard at a dead run. James pushed blindly into the woods, his shoulders scraping against the dark shadows of trees, feeling thorny vines tear at his jeans and golf shirt.

He heard a commotion that sounded like devils with giant wings trying to escape from the trees. Ahead of him in faint starlight he saw the ground drop away in a deep gully. The top of a small pine tree showed over the rim, and the branches were swaying wildly.

Erica screamed from somewhere in the gully.

James dived over the rim and landed hard on the exposed roots of a nearby oak. He flung out a hand and caught Erica's arm. She was huddled on the gully floor, and when he grabbed her she jumped like a rabbit.

Then she hit him across the stomach with a tree limb the size of a baseball bat.

He groaned. "Thanks."

"James!"

"No kidding."

He pushed her onto her side and curled around her spoon-style, one arm protectively flung across her head. They lay there panting and listened to the unknown terror in the pine tree.

Finally it got free of the limbs, emitted a ridiculous gobbling sound, and flew away on ponderous wings. James groaned again, this time in disgust.

"A damned turkey."

"A bird?" Erica asked in an apologetic tone.

The adrenaline surge ended, and pain rushed through James's bad knee. He bit his lip and rolled onto his back, then drew the knee up gingerly and described turkeys in terms that had nothing to do with Thanksgiving.

Erica sat up quickly. He could feel her scrutinizing him in the dark. "What—where are you hurt?" she asked anxiously.

"Bad knee," he said raspily. "Why I left pro ball."

"Oh, James." She patted her hands over him as if checking for concealed weapons. "Are you hurt somewhere else too?"

"Frisk a little lower and I'll pretend."

She exhaled in relief. "Wolfman, I salute your sense of humor, if not your priorities."

When he pushed himself into a sitting position, she knelt beside him, brushing leaves from his back and hair. His right leg throbbed. James squinted his eyes shut and wished that pain weren't radiating through all his erogenous zones.

Erica, naked and flustered, was fussing over him sympathetically. The ground was covered in a soft, thick cushion of leaves, the air smelled sweet with honeysuckle, and there was enough starlight to show the look on her face when he gently seduced her.

As if he needed to complicate an impossible situation. She was no more suited to life in these mountains than a swan was suited to life as a hawk. James grimaced. The injured knee was a blessing.

"Thank you for trying to protect me from the turkey," she murmured, her hands resting on his shoulder.

Feeling troubled, resenting the effect she had on him, James abruptly got to his feet and stood with the bad leg bent a little. "Rescuing virgins is no fun."

He heard her sharp intake of breath.

"Neither is being rescued from a turkey by a turkey."

"Follow me back to the damned house and don't give me any more grief."

He started climbing the gully wall, his movements slow and painful. Hurt like hell? Ignore it, his coaches had always said. He had to stop halfway up the gully to catch his breath.

Erica chuckled fiendishly. "I think I'm going to enjoy this."

"Red! Bring me a glass of water!"

"In a minute."

"Now."

"When I finish this chapter."

Sitting at the kitchen table, Erica lifted her gaze from a history book and smiled. For three days it had been that way—James in bed, bawling orders, her in the kitchen, ignoring them as long as possible.

She heard furious rustling in the living room, then uneven clumping. Alarmed, Erica put the book down and looked toward the kitchen door. James appeared in its whitewashed frame, his swollen knee half-bent, his hair disheveled, his eyes black with aggravation.

And he was naked.

Erica felt the pulse throb in her neck. She folded her hands in her lap to hide their trembling and said calmly, "Nice crutch."

He emphasized each word slowly. "From now on, every time you ignore me I'm going to get up, find you, and wave this thing until I get attention."

"You think I'm so mousey that I'll faint? Just because I've never had personal contact with one of those doesn't mean it terrifies me. It's just another part of the male body."

Her stomach shrank under his evil, slit-eyed smile. "Oh? Then you won't mind if it moves closer."

He hobbled toward her with a great deal more menace than she'd expected. Erica jumped up and sidled around the table, using it as a barricade.

To her chagrin, he began to laugh. He braced both hands on the tabletop and chortled heartily, his deep-set eyes squeezed almost shut, his teeth flashing white in an uninhibited show of victory.

Erica walked to the battered old metal sink, picked up a big glass from the drain rack, and filled it with water. She held her hand under the faucet for a moment. Mmmm, well water was so wonderfully cold. She turned gracefully, her chin up, and tossed the whole glass on him.

He jumped, knocked his bad knee on the table edge, and shot her a look of pain and exasperated shock. Water dripped from his eyebrows and nose; rivulets of water ran down the center of his sleek chest in a southward journey that ended in hair even blacker than that on his head.

To her amazement, the anger faded from his eyes. He sighed and shook his head. "This would have been a hell of a lot simpler two hundred years ago. I could have just kidnapped you."

Erica didn't know how to interpret that remark, but the possessive tone of it struck a wistful chord in her. "I'd have made a lousy captive," she said softly. "You'd have had to beat me a lot. You probably would have ended up trading me for a rusty gun and an old horse."

He frowned at her. "We didn't mistreat women and children, even captives. Most captives ended up being adopted by the tribe. And I'll tell you something else—we didn't buy or trade for our women. They chose their own husbands, and if they got tired of them, they kicked them out. The women in a village kept tabs on social conduct, and they'd gang up on any man who abused his family. From what I've read, they'd beat the crap out of him."

Erica couldn't help smiling. "Not a bad system."

"I thought you'd like it."

They gazed at each other while golden afternoon sunshine poured through a tiny window over the sink. It cascaded onto the table between them as if marking a common ground for friendship.

Erica was amazed at herself. She was calmly grinning at the most enticing man in the world, he was stark naked, and he was grinning back at her. Her life had certainly gotten more interesting in the course of one week.

"What are those marks on your chest?" she asked.

He glanced down. "Under my pecs?"

Somehow she hadn't expected to get this detailed. Erica thought he made "pecs" sound very sensual. "Under them, yes."

"Stretch marks. You get 'em from taking steroids. The steroids make your muscles grow faster than normal when you lift weights, and the skin can't take the stress." He paused, looking troubled. "In college we were proud of them."

"You can be proud of them now," she assured him gently. "Because you went through a lot of hell to do what you thought was right."

There was a vigorous change in attitude low on James's body. She couldn't help staring. Really, it was impossible not to. Erica's legs went weak, while a languid heat made her belly feel hollow and ready to be filled.

Would his body have reacted to any woman who stared at him? Erica shoved that worry aside.

James glanced down at himself and murmured distractedly, "Looks like I've got my own *Uktena*." Then he was silent, studying her reaction.

She whimpered silently as heat scorched the skin below her navel and moved higher, tightening her breasts until they ached, then finally warming her face with passion. Erica turned toward the sink and fumbled with some dishes there.

"Sorry about this," he said softly.

"I'm not embarrassed. I'm a normal woman with a normal reaction to a man in your . . . condition."

"I understand that. I'm just sorry, that's all."

She glanced back at him. He was scowling—if not at her, precisely, then in her general direction. He pursed his lips as if thinking, then turned and quickly limped out of the room.

"Would you mind bringing me some water when you get a chance, Red?"

"No problem."

"Thanks, doll."

Erica slumped in a chair and put her head in her hands. He didn't want her, even when she couldn't hide the fact that she was ready, able, and extremely willing. Lord, he must think she was the homeliest female this side of East Germany.

Erica wiped tears from her eyes. "Water," she said in a ragged, angry whisper. "There's your water, Mr. Tall Wolf."

Wrapped in a thin blanket, she sat cross-legged on the foot of the bed and listened to James tell stories. The bedside lamp cast cozy light on him, softening the planes of his face and making his hair look like polished onyx. He kept the bedcovers pulled up to his chest, which told her that he was politely avoiding another scene like that afternoon's.

Erica sighed. He had a lot of kindness in him, and that made her want him even more.

Beyond the living room windows owls "Whoo'd" in the June night, and inside, the house still smelled delicious from the steak dinner she'd fixed.

Erica pulled her blanket more tightly around herself. They'd had a wonderful dinner, and he was wonderful company. She should be content with that.

"How did the Tall Wolf family end up in North Carolina?" she asked. "How did they avoid the Trail of Tears?"

"My great-great-grandfather lived in Tennessee. When the soldiers began rounding up the Cherokees, he escaped and hid in North Carolina. Here in the Smokies." James smiled. "The *Tsacona-ge*. Place of the Blue Smoke."

"So most of the North Carolina band came from refugees?"

"Some. Others had lived here a long time, and the mountains were so rugged that it was too much trouble for the soldiers to hunt them down."

"Do you think your ancestor survived like the other refugees did, by hiding in caves?"

He nodded. "We have records made by a Quaker missionary."

"What kind of records?"

"Aw, that's not important. People nearly starved, hiding from the soldiers the first year, but then—"

"James, what kind of records?"

He looked annoyed at her persistence. "A family Bible."

"But why would the missionary record anything about your ancestor in his *family* Bible? Unless—" Erica whooped. "Did the big red wolf marry a little white lamb in the missionary's family?"

"Yeah, but—"

"Then you're part white. All right! We have something in common."

James crossed reddish-brown arms over his chest and feigned dismay. "Funny, I don't feel like a Quaker."

Erica clapped merrily. "Why does this subject bother you so much?"

"I'm proud to be Indian. I've never wanted to be white. Except for that one, ahem, Quaker incident, the Tall Wolf family is about as full-blooded as it gets."

Erica pulled her knees up and hugged them, trying to look nonchalant as she cut her eyes at him. "James, are you a bigot?"

"Antiwhite, you mean?"

"That's right, Wolfman."

"No. I'm pro-Indian."

"Don't you mean that you're pro-Indian *heritage*?"

"All right. Same difference."

"Nope. A person doesn't have to have a drop of Indian blood to claim the heritage. I bet my great-great-grandfather Justis was a terrific white Cherokee."

James pointed to himself. "You have to look the part to feel the difference."

Erica asked gently, "Has it been really bad, at times? Is there more prejudice than I realize?"

He nodded. "I'm not just talking about prejudice against me, personally—like college professors who automatically thought I'd be a bad student and parents who told me to stay away from their daughters—I'm talking important issues.

"We don't need handouts from the government. We need jobs. And teachers, we've gotta have teachers who understand that the old culture is just as important as the new."

"It's better now than it used to be, isn't it?"

"Oh, yeah. Only a few decades ago Cherokee kids would get punished at the reservation schools if they spoke their own language. Now a year of language and culture study is mandatory at the high school here. I can't read Cherokee, but at least I can speak it."

She rocked nonchalantly, smiling. "I understand that after you move back here for good you're going to find yourself a nice Cherokee wife."

"Hmmm. That's always been my plan."

"Keep the bloodline pure."

His gaze was riveted to hers; she wasn't certain what was going on behind those dark eyes, but she doubted it had anything to do with Erica Alice Gallatin's bloodlines.

"I just want to make sure my wife doesn't leave me," he told her in a low, measured voice. "And a Cherokee woman is a lot more likely to be happy on the reservation." He paused. "Travis's wife was white. Born and raised in Chicago. She left him five times. He always took her back. She made him miserable."

Erica looked at James wearily. The bitterness in his eyes defeated her. "I'm sorry. I like Travis, and it's too bad that his marriage didn't work. But maybe it had nothing to do with his wife's being white."

"You're right. It only had to do with her being an outsider."

Erica tried to sound flippant. "So you're just having fun with the palefaces until you find the right woman here at home. Hmmm, a practical attitude." She looked around as if searching for a clock. "Well, heavens, it's getting late. I must be off to my new bed. I'm so glad Tom's Trader Inn had one more lime-green beauty to spare."

Erica uncurled her legs and started to get up. James's broad hand latched on to her ankle.

"Not so fast. You owe me a story in return."

She had to get out of that room before her smile broke. Not only wasn't she sexy enough for him, she wasn't Indian enough.

"Well, let's see, I know a story about the great Boston Harbor sewage monster, but I don't think it's as charming as your stories about *Uktenas* and *Utluhtus* and other Indian things that go bump in the night."

"I want to know about your marriage."

"Ah. No. I've read that Indians have a tendency toward diabetes, and the story's too darned sweet to be safe."

"Red, quit stalling," he said softly. "I can keep a secret. Come on. Give."

"Really, it's a ridiculous story and I don't want to—"

"Erica Alice, I'm not letting go of your ankle until you talk."

She resettled herself and wrapped the blanket even more tightly around her shoulders. "You're not kidding," she said grimly.

"You heap right, paleface."

"Check your blood sugar level," she murmured. Erica stared at her blanket and tried to forget that James was watching every expression on her face.

"I was a nerd; he was a nerd. We dated all through high school. It was a terrific nerd romance. Then I went to Georgia Tech to study civil engineering and he went to UCLA to study world arts and cultures.

"We hardly saw each other for four years, but we wrote lots of long letters full of deathless prose about making the world into a better place. Then he got a chance to visit the Middle East on a year-long study program. On his way out of the States he met me up in Boston. He made me feel as if no one would ever love me more in my life. We were married an hour before he got on an airplane."

She picked at the blanket for a second. "And that was the last time I ever saw him in person."

James stroked her ankle. "What happened?"

"He disappeared. The State Department confirmed that he'd been kidnapped by some political faction. I saw photographs of him over the years, so I knew he was still alive."

"So you waited," James murmured. "For eight years before you found out that he was dead. My God, you're incredible."

"I'm a dolt," she retorted, and chuckled harshly. "He wasn't dead. He wasn't even kidnapped. He'd joined a terrorist group and married a Lebanese woman. At last count, they had three kids."

She sat in awkward silence, toying with a string on the blanket. James's hand tightened around her ankle as if he wanted to stamp his fingerprints permanently on her skin. Erica avoided looking at him even when he shook her foot lightly.

"What'd you do when you found out?" he asked in a husky voice that played havoc with her emotions. This forceful giant of a man might growl and snap at her sometimes, but he could be as sweet as a puppy, too. A wolf puppy, but a puppy, nonetheless.

Blinking back tears, Erica could only manage to repeat, "I was a damned dolt. What a boob. Eight years."

"Sssh. You ought to get a medal."

"An idiot award."

"Hush. When did you find out about him?"

"About two years ago. I got an annulment and tried to think of myself as a free person, but it hasn't worked real well. I guess eight years of martyrdom turned me into a creature of habit. And I'm not exactly self-confident around men . . . except in business."

"Dammit, you can't waste any more time." He cursed again, this time less politely. "What a story. The guy ought to be barbecued."

She almost smiled. "I've often thought about which parts I'd like to roast first."

James looked at her shrewdly. "So what are you going to do? Let that bastard ruin the rest of your life?"

"No, but—"

"What are you waiting for?"

"I—I guess it's a who, not a what."

"No, no, no. You can't sit around waiting for Mr. Perfect and ignoring everyone else. You'll never get anywhere that way."

Erica looked at him hopefully, her heart filling her throat. Was he making an offer?

"I don't need romance," she said eagerly. "I mean, I know I'm not the type that men get mushy over. Guys just don't pamper big women. We don't look delicate. If I could find someone who's experienced but not too cynical, someone who could be a good friend, someone who, you know, would teach me things, I'd be happy."

James frowned at her. "You need a lot more than sex education. You need a new self-image. Don't worry about being too tall to attract men. Take me, for example. I'm such a hulk that you look delicate to me."

Happiness bubbled up inside her. He *was* making her an offer. "You're good for my ego," she said, and laughed merrily. "I feel like Eliza in *My Fair Lady*. Make me a new woman, Henry Tall Wolf Higgins."

"Let's see, let's see." He squinted thoughtfully, his fingers tapping on her ankle.

"Tell me what to do, and I'll give it a try."

"Hmmm. Okay, I've got it." He didn't look particularly happy, but he did seem satisfied.

Erica leaned forward, waiting breathlessly. "Anything."

He patted her ankle. "I know a great guy up in D.C. Used to play for the 'Skins. He's divorced, but it was nothing ugly. He's real clean-cut, a little shy, not nearly as bookish or smart as you are, but he does read a lot. He's a liberal Republican. I think you'd like him."

For a second Erica could only stare at James, her mouth open in disbelief. Her chest constricted with stunned bitterness. After years of idiotic martyrdom and self-denial she'd been forced into close company with this man, this incredibly provocative man, and all he wanted to do was get rid of her.

"What's a liberal Republican?" she asked in a low, sardonic tone. "Someone who believes in equal opportunity for millionaires?"

James studied her expression, and when he saw the fury in it, he looked surprised. "Do the guy's politics make that much difference to you?"

Erica seethed. "Are you dense? I don't care about his politics!" She clambered off the bed and stood at the foot of it, her hands clenched around her blanket, her feet braced apart in a stance of pure defiance. "I don't need you to pimp for me!"

He drew a slow breath. It expanded his broad chest and lifted his head majestically, as if filling a human balloon. In fact, he looked as though he'd been overinflated and might burst.

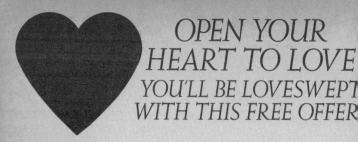

# OPEN YOUR HEART TO LOVE
## YOU'LL BE LOVESWEPT WITH THIS FREE OFFER

## HERE'S WHAT YOU GET:

**1.** **FREE!** SIX NEW LOVESWEPT NOVELS! You get 6 beautiful stories filled with passion, romance, laughter, and tears...exciting romances to stir the excitement of falling in love... again and again.

**2.** **FREE!** A BEAUTIFUL MAKEUP CASE WITH A MIRROR THAT LIGHTS UP! What could be more useful than a makeup case with a mirror that lights up\*? Once you open the tortoise-shell finish case, you have a choice of brushes...for your lips, your eyes, and your blushing cheeks.

\*(batteries not included)

**3.** **SAVE!** MONEY-SAVING HOME DELIVERY! Join the Loveswept at-home reader service and we'll send you 6 new novels each month. You always get 15 days to preview them before you decide. Each book is yours for only $2.09 — a savings of 41¢ per book.

**4.** **BEAT THE CROWDS!** You'll always receive your Loveswept books before they are available in bookstores. You'll be the first to thrill to these exciting new stories.

BE LOVESWEPT TODAY — JUST COMPLETE, DETACH AND MAIL YOUR FREE-OFFER CARD.

# FREE–LIGHTED MAKEUP CASE!
# FREE–6 LOVESWEPT NOVELS!

- NO OBLIGATION
- NO PURCHASE NECESSARY

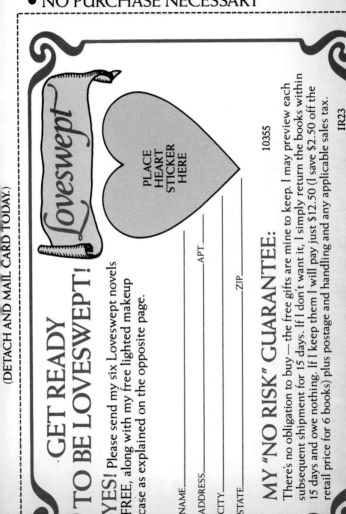

(DETACH AND MAIL CARD TODAY.)

## GET READY TO BE LOVESWEPT!

**YES!** Please send my six Loveswept novels FREE, along with my free lighted makeup case as explained on the opposite page.

PLACE HEART STICKER HERE

NAME _____

ADDRESS _____ APT. _____

CITY _____

STATE _____ ZIP _____

10355

## MY "NO RISK" GUARANTEE:

There's no obligation to buy — the free gifts are mine to keep. I may preview each subsequent shipment for 15 days. If I don't want it, I simply return the books within 15 days and owe nothing. If I keep them I will pay just $12.50 (I save $2.50 off the retail price for 6 books) plus postage and handling and any applicable sales tax.

IR23

# REMEMBER!

- The free books and gift are mine to keep!
- There is no obligation!
- I may preview each shipment for 15 days!
- I can cancel anytime!

"Pimp?" he echoed in a dangerous tone, his eyes narrowed. "I try to help you and you call me that?"

"I'm not some kind of pitiful creature who needs matchmakers and blind dates."

He shoved himself forward in bed and jabbed a finger at her. "Women like you give old maids a bad name."

"You must have the vocabulary of a turnip. *Old maid* and *virgin* seem to be the only words you know."

"You said them first. If that's the way you define yourself, I'm not going to argue any more."

Erica figured she had about two sentences left before she started to cry with rage. They'd better be good ones. "I'll teach you some new words," she said crisply. "Like pride, self-control, and morals."

"Don't forget saint, stubborn, and smartass."

She turned and marched from the room, her dignity in tatters around her.

# *Six*

The next morning at six A.M. he pounded on her bedroom door and called, "Wake up, *kamama egwa*."

Erica refused to ask what the name meant. She sat up wearily, still angry and tense. "Yes?"

"I'm going out. Meet me at the museum at twelve."

"Why?"

"We're going on a hike. Wear comfortable shoes."

"Where are we going?"

"And don't eat lunch. We'll go native in the woods."

Frustrated, Erica sank both hands into her hair and groaned softly. Native. "I'm not taking my clothes off to eat lunch. *Where are we going?*"

"Be there," he said firmly, and she listened to him leave the house. He still had a slight limp, so they couldn't be hiking far.

Erica fell back on the bed and stared at a ceiling made of thick boards painted pale blue. Dove had certainly loved blue; most of the colors in the house were some variety of the color. It was soothing, and she needed soothing just then.

She suspected she was going to need it more as the day went on.

Erica drove over to Asheville after breakfast and turned in her rental car, then went to a used-truck dealer and drolly leased a Jeep Cherokee. As she drove back along a winding road perched on the sides of mountains, she blessed the Jeep's oversized tires and four-wheel drive.

She rolled down her window, let the fragrant spring breeze wash over her, and slipped a Cherokee-language cassette into the Jeep's tape player. She'd mail-ordered the tape from the reservation in Oklahoma, and the dialect differed significantly from that used in North Carolina, but she could still benefit from it.

She smiled as she went through the tape, feeling very Cherokee as she repeated phrases and words. '*Egwa*. Big." Erica gritted her teeth. James had called her *kamama egwa*. Something big. Whatever it was, it couldn't be good.

After that she didn't smile.

Eventually she reached the sign that marked the reservation's eastern border. "*Qualla Boundary*, she read aloud. She didn't know what *Qualla* meant, but it sounded homey. A few minutes later Erica slowed the Jeep as woodland gave way to billboards and the road became crowded with tourist traffic.

She turned off the tape as she entered Cherokee. Gazing out at the tourist district, Erica cataloged the offerings—the Sequoyah Cafeteria, the Papoose Motel, the Pow Wow Gift Shop, an amusement park called Santa's Land, and dozens of other attractions.

In contrast, Becky Tall Wolf's little restaurant was simply called, Mama's Best Meal, and, judging by the early lunch crowd, it was a success. Erica had to stop at crosswalks to let hordes of camera-toting families pass.

As she sat waiting she glanced at the storefronts. Before one stood a middle-aged Cherokee man in full chief's costume—beaded moccasins, fringed buckskins, and a huge feathered war bonnet. A large sign was propped on a porch post beside him.

"Take a photograph with Chief Running Bear. And don't forget to tip!"

She sighed. On the reservation this occupation was called "chiefing." The costumes were strictly Plains Indian style, and more Hollywood than authentic, at that. But still, it was a job, and from what she'd heard the men who did it worked long, hard hours. Even when the public was obnoxious they demonstrated an incredible amount of courtesy and showmanship.

Farther down Erica stopped at another crosswalk. This time when she looked over at the shops she gasped in surprise.

Grandpa Sam was chiefing.

She pulled into one of the slanted parking spaces that fronted the stores and hurried over to Sam's spot. He held a squalling toddler in one arm while the mother stood beside him uncertainly and the father snapped pictures with an expensive-looking camera.

Erica winced. Grandpa Sam had braided his long white hair into two plaits that hung down over his shoulders, onto his chest, and decorated them with orange feathers.

Still, dressed in a headdress that hung to his heels and wearing a beaded buckskin outfit made by an obviously loving hand, he brought dignity to the costume.

As the family walked away Sam called cheerfully, "Have a good stay in Cherokee!" He turned, saw Erica watching, and grinned. "Howdy do, *Eh-lee-ga.*"

She smiled with fascination. "Is that how you say my name in Cherokee?"

He nodded. "Eh-lee-ga. We got no 'r' sound."

"Mr. Tall Wolf—"

"Call me Grandpa Sam. You're one of us, the *Ani-Yun-Wiya,* the Real People, and all of them call me Grandpa."

Erica thought her chest would burst with affection. "Thank you, Grandpa Sam," she said around a knot in her throat.

"What you doin' today?"

She told him about going to the museum to meet

James. As she did, his gaze strayed across the street. Suddenly he muttered, "I'll be damned. Quicker than flies after a dead horse."

Erica glanced over. A competing chief, this one short and plump, with a face like a Cherokee Buddha, was holding a toddler in *his* arms. He gave Sam a thumbs-up.

"Copies me 'cause he's too dumb to think up things on his own," Sam grumbled.

Erica bit her lip to keep from laughing. "Do you do this every day?"

The majestic war bonnet nodded solemnly. "Make good money at it, most days. Mainly do it 'cause I like to keep busy and meet people." He thumped his chest. "I've had my picture made with people from all over the world, and some of 'em write me letters when they get home. I'm on ten different postcards, too." Sam cupped a hand beside his mouth and said in a low voice, "Don't mention I said so, but Germans tip better than Americans."

Erica clasped her hands behind her back and asked casually, "Grandpa Sam, what does *kamama* mean?"

"Hmmm. It means butterfly."

Erica gazed up at him in surprise. "If somebody called me a big butterfly, would it be a compliment?"

He looked mischievous. "Yes. Who called you that?" When she shifted a little and smiled ruefully, he clucked his tongue. "That James," Sam murmured. "He's a caution."

Erica nodded, a dull lump in her stomach. *Caution* was the appropriate word.

Out of the corner of one eye Erica spotted James crossing the museum floor toward her. He was waylaid by an elderly museum worker who apparently knew him. She squealed and grabbed his hand, then began to talk.

The giant standing near Erica took that moment to speak to her for the first time. "Pardon me," he said politely in a voice as deep as mountain thunder. "May I ask you a question?"

Erica turned toward him, tilted her head far back, and looked at a rugged, attractive face topped by black hair. But it wasn't Indian-black, and neither his features nor his coloring indicated any Indian blood. Her neck ached from looking up. Lord, he was seven feet tall. Was there some sort of magic-growth elixir around there?

"Yes?"

"I saw you in the bookstore talking to the cashier. Is she a friend of yours?"

That was Echo. Hmmm. What did this black-haired Atlas want with James's sister? "Yes, she's a friend."

"Is she married?"

"Uhmm, no." Erica squinted at him shrewdly. There was a worldliness about his dark eyes that made her feel he was much more sophisticated than his questions made him sound. She glanced at his tan corduroy trousers, short-sleeved khaki safari shirt, and well-used hiking shoes.

"Who are you, and why do you want to know about her?"

He thought for a moment, then leaned close to her ear and murmured, "I noticed in the guest book that your name is Erica Gallatin. Do you have a relative named Tess?"

Erica drew back in astonishment. "Yes."

"I'm a neighbor of hers. Drake Lancaster. Call her in California and check me out."

That sounded legitimate. Erica gestured vaguely around them. "But how—"

"I work for the forestry service, and I'm based in Los Angeles. I'm doing some pollution research over in the Nantahala area, a few miles west of here."

"But how—"

"I keep a sailboat at the marina where Tess lives. At Long Beach."

"Ah!" Well, amazing as this coincidence was, he *did*

know indisputable details about her cousin. Erica was still stunned, but she held out a hand. "Hello, then."

He shook gently so his large paw wouldn't crush her fingers. "Now, about the cashier. I want to buy some books, and then I want her to go to lunch with me. Will you help me out?"

Erica had been glancing at James, and she enjoyed the way he kept glancing at her and the giant. She took Drake Lancaster's hand again. "If you'll do me a favor I'll introduce you to the cashier and tell her you're a friend of my cousin's."

His dark eyes gleamed with pleasure at the intrigue. "All right."

"Put your arm around me. Pretend we're old pals from college. This won't get you in trouble, I promise."

He smiled slowly. "That's all right. Trouble doesn't bother me."

He might have been shy, but he wasn't awkward. Gracefully he slipped a massive arm around her waist and pulled her close to his side. "Just old friends?"

"Right." Erica smiled at James. He arched one brow but continued talking to the museum worker. She lifted a hand and waved casually. Drake Lancaster followed the direction. He smiled and nodded to James before looking down at her again. "Now what?"

"You went to Georgia Tech. Studied . . . hmmm, biology. Yeah, that ties in with your job. I was a little sister in your fraternity—"

"Whoa," he said, chuckling. "When you make up an identity, keep it simple. It works better that way."

She looked at him quizzically, wondering how a biologist would have experience with such things. James's appearance beside her made her forget that thought. Erica grinned at him and pointed to Drake. "An old college friend."

She patted Drake's chest and smiled up at him. "I can't believe it's been so many years."

He squeezed her waist companionably. "We had some good times. I've never forgotten."

Lord, this man was a wonderful accomplice. Erica smiled at James, who was doing a good job of looking inscrutable.

"Drake Lancaster, meet James Tall Wolf. James is helping me do some research on a relative of mine."

James shook the giant's hand and smiled pleasantly at him. "You went to Georgia Tech with Erica?"

"Sure did."

"He studied biology," Erica chimed in. "And now he works for the forestry service."

James arched a brow. "Did you play football?"

"Oh, yes," Erica interjected. She looked up hopefully at Drake Lancaster.

There was a hint of exasperation in his eyes, but he chuckled. "Sure did."

"What position?"

Drake never missed a beat. "Defensive end."

"Hmmm. Well, glad to meet you." James looked from Drake to her and smiled with a nonchalance that made her heart sink. He didn't care if she knew a dozen giant, good-looking men. "Ready for lunch?"

Erica shrugged. "Sure. But I want to introduce Drake to Echo first. Umm, Drake knows my cousin Tess, by the way. Tess, from California."

"Go ahead. I'll be waiting." He shook Drake's hand again, then sat down on a cushioned bench and yawned.

Erica grimly led Drake Lancaster to the museum bookstore. "Thank you," she told him. "You did all you could."

The bookstore was empty of customers; Echo had her back to the door, and she was rearranging books on a big display rack, one that rotated.

Erica glanced at Drake Lancaster and was fascinated by the intense way he studied a woman to whom he hadn't yet spoken. But of course Echo was beautiful, in addition to being six two and having an incredible mane of black hair. She wore deerskin ankle boots, soft cotton pants, and a ruffled blouse that made her look very feminine.

Wonderfully feminine, but not delicate. Erica recalled that Echo, in her spare time, was a blacksmith.

Echo grabbed the rotating rack, hoisted the whole thing off the floor and easily carried it to a spot in one corner. Drake Lancaster leaped forward to help her but arrived just as she plopped the rack into place.

He grasped her elbow. "That was impressive," he said with utter sincerity. "You must have strong hands."

Echo jumped, looked up, and simply stared at Drake in open-mouthed wonder. Erica stopped a few feet away and watched wistfully as an almost visible form of energy passed between the two of them.

She sighed, thinking of James waiting for her in the museum without an ounce of jealousy or interest. Well, if she couldn't find romance for herself, at least she'd find it for other people.

"Echo," she said softly, watching the hypnotized look in her eyes, "this gentleman wants to talk to you."

James guided her to Grandpa Sam's old pickup truck. He kept a benevolent silence as he drove along a pleasant, almost suburban street paralleled by a tree-shadowed river. He pointed to it. "Oconaluftee," he noted.

"Gesundheit."

He chuckled. They passed the ceremonial grounds, the tribal council house, and a small, neatly kept building that housed the Bureau of Indian Affairs. James cut across the river and turned down another road.

Erica gazed out the passenger window as they passed a large, impressive brick building. A fire truck and other official vehicles sat out front. "How's Travis?" she asked abruptly. "You don't say much about him."

"We don't have much to say to each other."

Erica looked at James quickly. His wide, firm mouth had thinned a little, and the pain around his eyes couldn't be hidden. She'd spent several days watching this man try to ignore the pain in his knee, and so she recognized the different type of pain in him now.

"Anything you want to talk about?" she asked.

"I told his wife I'd set her up in a house in Chicago if she'd divorce Travis and stay away for good."

"Oh, James," Erica said sadly.

"I guess I sound like a real SOB."

"I don't know. Were you doing it for Travis?"

"Yeah. After she left him the fifth time. Father and Grandfather tracked Travis up to the top of Rattlesnake Mountain—it's a sacred place in the old legends—and they found him sitting there with a gun in his hands. I don't know what he would have done to himself if they hadn't brought him back home. When I heard what almost happened, I knew I couldn't let my brother get to that point again."

Erica let her breath out. "You're a good brother, not an SOB."

"Don't ask Travis for an opinion."

"I doubt that he's stopped loving you. He sounds like a man who loves with great loyalty."

"I hope so. It's a tradition with us wolves."

Erica turned her face so he couldn't see her expression. "So once you take a mate, it's for life, eh?"

"We try to work it out that way."

"Good plan." She was silent as he drove out of town and into the steep hills. "Where are we going?"

His voice was wicked. "To a wolf's cave."

James moved the leather bag from one shoulder to another and favored his bad knee. The trail wasn't as steep as he remembered, but he was glad he had Erica along as an excuse to go slowly.

"Tired yet?" he called over his shoulder. He could imagine her behind him, her face flushed with exertion, her T-shirt clinging to her breasts, her jeans just damp enough to mold more intimately to her city-bred legs.

Actually, a tired Erica might be the most seductive sight in the world. When she didn't answer, he stopped and turned around to look. She was down the trail, picking wild flowers.

"I'm coming!" she called, and bounded up the slope with the energy of a young deer. She halted a step away from him and tucked a cluster of tiny blue blossoms above one ear. "Ready," she said enthusiastically.

James couldn't imagine anything prettier than the way she looked up at him, her green eyes flashing happiness. "Are you enjoying yourself?" he asked.

She nodded. "I feel like a carefree elf." She laughed. "Elf's not the best description, maybe." Dropping her chin a little, she looked at him from under her eyebrows. "Maybe I feel like a big butterfly."

"Hmmm." He almost grinned at her. She'd wasted no time finding someone to translate his words, and he admired her tenacity. That was the problem—he admired everything about her, and the night before, his throat had felt scalded when he'd offered to set her up with another man.

But dammit, though she was definitely different from any other outside woman he'd known, though she was part Cherokee, she wasn't suited to live in these mountains with him.

James felt a stab of embarrassment at his arrogance. Who said she wanted to live with him? She needed someone to teach her in bed, and she knew he could do it. He was exotic and dangerous in a way that excited her. But those kind of fireworks didn't last.

"Keep your wings moving, *kamama egwa*," he said sternly. "Don't stop to smell the flowers."

She pointed to the bag. "Is that lunch?"

"Not unless you like to gnaw leather."

She chortled. "No, thanks. I remember those steaks you grilled the other night."

"I like my meat well done."

"Me too, but I hate to leave my teeth in it." She curled her lips inward to feign toothlessness. "Gwate dinner, Dames."

He choked on amusement, gave up, and laughed

loudly. When he finished she was looking at him as if he were a tasty blossom and she were hungry for a sip of nectar. She quickly turned her gaze away, cleared her throat, and pointed.

"Is that pretty bald ridge anything special in tribal myths?"

James gazed at graceful summits capped by wind-carved granite. "The *Nuhnehi* have a council house there. Underground. They're immortals who look like Cherokees—if they decide to let themselves be seen. They usually stay invisible."

"Are they friendly?"

"Yeah. In the old days they'd come out and help us in battle." He paused. "You mentioned elves. We have elves. We call them *Yunwi Tsunsdi*, the Little People. They live all over the place up here. They're possessive about the mountains, and they can be mischievous if you get on their bad side."

He gestured toward her flowers. "Better thank them for using their pretties."

Her eyes glowed with interest. James watched as she slowly turned in a circle, gazing at the forest around her. "Thank you, *Yunwi Tsunsdi*. You have a beautiful home."

James sighed grandly. "I hope that satisfies them. I'd hate to have a cranky elf punch my bad knee."

Smiling at each other, they continued upward.

Thirty minutes later they reached a magnificent over-hang of silver-gray rock. In front of it was a view of misty mountains gleaming blue-green in the sunlight. Under it was a cave about twenty feet deep, with a ceiling just high enough for James to walk beneath without bending.

They entered the shadowy coolness and gazed at walls etched with Cherokee letters. "This is where my great-great-great-grandfather hid from the soldiers," James said softly. "Over one hundred and fifty years ago."

Erica went to a wall, knelt, and reverently touched letters of a more familiar kind. "Amanda and James," she read. When she looked up at James urgently, he knew he had to explain.

"I was named after him."

"And Amanda was the Quaker missionary's daughter?"

"Yes."

"She came up here and hid with him?"

"That's what we think. Nobody's sure. Grandpa says he remembers old stories that say she ran away from home to be with James against her parents' wishes."

Erica looked around sympathetically. "She must have suffered up here in the wintertime. They both must have." She gazed at him with a jaunty tilt to her head. "So the only other James Tall Wolf in the family loved a proper but strong-willed white woman."

James cast a troubled frown at her. Why had he brought her there? He'd simply wanted to show her how rough life had been for his ancestors, to give her a feeling for the past. Or was that all?

Suddenly he felt that he'd tricked himself into a dangerous situation, that forces beyond his conscious will were making him do reckless things.

James resisted the urge to look around for Little People. "Time for lunch," he announced.

Erica rose, her eyes never leaving him. He knelt at the cave entrance and opened the leather bag, all the while feeling her provocative gaze on him.

"Why did you bring me here?" she asked.

He gave her the safe explanation he'd given himself. She sat down next to him, crossed her legs, and propped her chin on one hand. "Thank you for sharing this with me," she murmured softly. "It means a lot to me."

James looked at her and felt a disastrous urge simply to surrender to the affection in those green eyes. He'd make love to her right there in that lonely, beautiful cave where the Tall Wolf family had begun so long ago. He'd bond her to him with her love for Cherokee history and her need for his touch.

His hand trembled on the leather bag, then gripped it hard. And when she left him, he might be as Travis had been, lost and self-destructive with grief over a woman who'd never been destined to stay with him.

James said gruffly, "So your good buddy Drake was a defensive end at Tech, huh?"

He saw the light fade from her eyes. She smiled innocently and shrugged. "Yep."

James leaned forward, scrutinized her hard enough to make her blink a few times, and said softly, "Doll, I'd have heard about a monster like him if he'd played defense at a college as important as Tech. Drake Lancaster sure as hell never did."

Her shoulders slumped. "Right," she said grimly. "I made it up."

"The whole thing?"

"The whole thing. I met him about a minute before you walked in the room." She lifted her chin and looked haughty. "You're not the only one who can play games."

Lord, how he loved this woman's spirit. If she botched things up, she simply admitted it and took the consequences. And what were the consequences? She'd been trying to make him jealous, and he'd never tell her how well it had been working before she'd made that revealing comment about Lancaster's playing football.

"Why did you do it?" James demanded. He knew the real reason, but he had to hear the official one.

"To show you that I'm no wimp around men," she retorted. "Now, go ahead and be annoyed, if you want to. I'm annoyed at myself. I'm not accustomed to stooping to such childish pranks."

James opened the bag and pulled out a shelled acorn. "Any woman who attacks me with a hand drill, hits me with a stick, then throws cold water on me when I'm naked is no wimp."

She looked startled by his good humor; then the affection came flooding back into her eyes. James almost groaned out loud.

"Eat," he ordered, and popped the acorn into her mouth.

She squinted unhappily and chewed. "Ugh."

"That's what I'm supposed to say."

"What are we having for lunch?"

"Nature's own. Nuts, roots, unsalted beef jerky, and dried corn. I wanted you to eat the same foods people had to live on when they were hiding in the caves around here."

Almost as an afterthought he pulled out a small swollen bag. "Water bag," he told her, and smiled fiendishly. "Made from deer bladder. Mmmm. Gives the water a nice, musky taste."

She sniffed quaintly and cut her eyes at him. "Why, at home I have a whole set of deer-bladder water bags to go with my fine china. With my initials on them."

James gave up and gazed at her with a broad smile. She picked up a root, chomped it like a carrot, and said jauntily, "You and I are friends. Nope, you can't deny it anymore. You want it too. Pals. And because we know it's never going to be any more than that, we can relax, okay?"

He felt bittersweet sorrow gather inside his chest like an empty mountain valley filling with blue mist.

"Okay," he agreed solemnly, and sat back wondering why victory had never tasted less sweet.

# *Seven*

Erica rocked slowly in her chair and peered at an article in the quarterly history journal published by the tribe.

James lay on the porch near her feet, his head propped on a pillow. He was a very languid-looking wolf as he studied her medallion and awkwardly tried to copy the symbols onto a note pad that lay on his chest. Erica glanced at him, then glanced away, sighing at his effect on her heart rate.

They'd had a lovely friendship for three days; except for her constant state of lovesickness she thought the arrangement worked well.

More than ever he wanted to keep it platonic, judging by his sudden decision to dress like a character from Li'l Abner. He wore faded overalls sans shirt or shoes, he ruffled his hair and let its straight black strands do what they wanted, he smoked a long cigar every night after dinner, and he tromped around with grass stains on his feet.

Erica smiled ruefully. He thought he looked ugly to her that way.

Didn't he know that overalls exposed a tantalizing expanse of his chest and shoulders and that there was something wonderfully indecent about the way they pulled tightly across his muscular rump? He also didn't

realize that she loved the scent of cigars, because her
father had smoked them, and the fragrance brought
back warm feelings of happiness.

Erica smiled helplessly. James's hair shagged over
his forehead in a handsome way when he didn't brush
it, and his bare feet were big, knotty, cute-ugly things.

"I wonder if my great-great-grandmother had to go
on the Trail of Tears. It was worse than I ever imagined. Listen to this, Wolfman."

"Hmmm?" he mumbled, and looked up at her. Erica
snapped her mouth shut—half the time she felt like a
slack-jawed trout around him—and went back to
reading.

"Here's the reprint of a letter written by an elderly
lady who was a teenager at the time the Cherokees
were removed to Oklahoma.

There was a woman of the Blue Clan who knew
white people's medicine. Her name was Katlanicha.
She doctored people on the trail, but could not
help so many who died from hunger and fever.
We called her *Ghighau*, Beloved Woman. A white
man came and stole the Beloved Woman one night.
Our people chased him, but his horse was too fast.
There was great sadness in the camp. I don't know
what happened to the Beloved Woman. She was
very pretty, and the man probably sold her. Sometimes that happened to pretty Cherokee women.

Erica put the journal down and stared into space,
thinking. "What an awful fate. Sold into some kind of
bondage, I bet. Maybe to a bordello."

"Think positive. Maybe she escaped."

"I hope so. Poor woman." She looked at him specula-
tively. "Have you ever visited a bordello?"

He stopped writing and gazed at her in astonish-

ment. Then he groaned. "No! Erica Alice, you can surprise the warts off a frog."

She grinned. "I just wanted a yes or no."

"You just wanted to provoke me. I'm not that kind of
man, and you know it. If you really thought I was so
low-class, you wouldn't be here."

Erica thought he'd figured her out too well. It was
time for another offensive to distract him. "Okay, that's
true. I'm being serious now—and I'm not trying to
upset you. I honestly want to know—what's it like to
make love to strangers?"

He dropped the medallion. For a second he just stared
at her in disbelief. Then he shook his head. "That was
something I did when I was young and stupid. Now
when I make love to a woman she's someone I know as
a friend, too. And there aren't many of those. Believe it.
Amazing as it may sound to you, it's true."

*A friend.* But not a friend like her, apparently. Erica
gripped the arms of the rocking chair and tried to look
cheerful.

"Good. I knew you were just joking that night in D.C.
Because we were strangers. You know, in the elevator."

His expression darkened. "Right."

Erica picked up her journal and gazed at it stead-
fastly. Okay, she'd wanted to confirm her worst suspi-
cion, and she had. No question about it—his ardor had
been a fluke, a basic masculine response to kissing a
woman and being kissed back.

She turned a page and murmured distractedly, "I'm
glad we got that misunderstanding straight." The word
he said next made her gaze at him in feigned shock.
"Why, sir, I haven't heard such language since a sub-
contractor dropped a sink on my foot."

He tossed her the medallion and the pad. "I never
knew how talkative big butterflies could be," he said,
grumbling, and started indoors.

The sound of a car made them both look toward the
driveway. Echo's deluxe station wagon rolled into sight.

"Nice wheels," Erica said. "Wonder what ex-football

player with lots of money gave it to her for her birthday last year?" She gazed up at James as he came to stand beside her chair. "You're a sweet guy, even if you do talk dirty to old maids."

He tried to resist, but finally he smiled at her nonsense. "You love it."

Echo parked and got out, moving wearily. Her hair was carelessly braided down her back, and she wore a rumpled sundress with old tennis shoes. Erica studied her anxiously, and when she glanced up at James, he looked worried too.

"Hi," Echo said as she walked to the porch. "I need to talk."

"Here, sit down." Erica moved to the floor.

James hugged his sister and looked shrewdly at her pinched face. "It's about Lancaster," he said grimly.

She lifted her chin and frowned at James in warning. "I love him. I know he's an outsider and we haven't known each other long, but don't say it's a mistake."

To Erica's surprise James only squeezed her shoulders and said, "I understand. It happens that way sometimes."

Erica buried her anguish behind a stoic mask. He spoke with such experience. Whom had he loved so deeply and so quickly?

He guided Echo to the chair and sat down at her feet, his legs crossed. "What is it, sis?"

But Echo had turned her attention to Erica. "What else do you know about Drake Lancaster? Anything besides what he told you the other day?"

Erica shook her head. "Do you suspect that he's not telling the truth? I know what he said about my cousin Tess is true."

Echo rubbed tired eyes. "All I know is that yesterday he took a pack horse and rode up into the national forest. And when he came back the pack horse had been unloaded. He goes off by himself for about fifteen minutes every afternoon at six. He's renting a room over near the Nantahala outfitters—one of those places where people stay while they kayak on the Nantahala River. But he won't let me visit it. Says it's too cheap, too messy."

James looked a little perturbed at the idea of his little sister, though full grown and previously married, visiting a man's room. But he said without rebuke, "So where do you go?"

Echo looked just as perturbed. She cleared her throat. "He took a better room over at one of the inns. But he kept the other room. It doesn't make sense. And he won't talk about his research at all. Says it's dull. Doesn't that strike you as odd?"

Erica sighed with resignation. "Yes, and I'm afraid something else is odd." She told Echo about Drake's confident way of handling false identities.

Echo put her head in her hands and made a soft sound of despair. "I'm afraid he's into something illegal," she said wretchedly. "Maybe drug running? I don't know." When she looked up there were tears on her face. "And he says he loves me, but I think he's got someone else."

James vaulted to his feet and began to pace. "What makes you say that, sis?" he asked in a lethal tone.

"He . . ." Echo swallowed hard and looked at Erica for moral support. Erica reached out and took her hand. "In one of his tote bags I found a brand-new bra. One of those really racy, see-through things. Not my size. It was a gift for someone. It had a pink bow tied to one strap. And I found a box of condoms with a blue bow tied around it."

"Maybe he's invited to a, ummm, coed bachelor party," Erica said lamely.

Echo shook her head. "He's a loner. He says he doesn't need to know anyone around here except me."

James stopped by the chair and looked down at her, a muscle flexing in his jaw. "Tell me what you want me to do, and I'll do it. That's what big brothers are for. I'll go talk to this character—"

Echo gasped. "James, I love you dearly, but I don't

want you to fight my battles. I just hoped that you and Erica would have some advice. I mean, you two are from the outside. You've both had a lot of experience with relationships."

James pursed his lips and gazed at Erica solemnly. "Red? What kind of advice do you have?"

Erica thought she'd enjoy taking the drill to him after Echo left. "Well, I believe in honesty. You should just go to Drake and tell him you want the truth."

"Or your brothers will help him reenact Custer's Last Mistake," James added. "With the obvious ending."

Echo wiped her eyes and managed to smile. "At least you and Travis finally agree on something. He said the same thing."

Erica watched quiet pleasure darken James's eyes. "Good," he said gruffly.

Echo looked from him to Erica. "I think you should know. People are talking about you two. Of course, Becky and Grandpa and I just ignore it, but we'd like to know what the, ummm, arrangement is here."

Erica smiled brightly. "We have a very modern relationship. We're just housemates and friends."

"Ah-hah." Echo looked at her askance, as if James had never had such a rare animal in his possession before.

"What are people saying?" James asked, his eyes troubled.

"Honesty." Echo exhaled as if the word were a burden. "The most interesting rumor is that Erica's pregnant and she's hiding here until she has the baby, because you don't want to marry her. But James, you remember how it is around here. People gossip just to have something to do. And you're big news. It'll pass. Becky and I'll work on it."

Erica's heart sank as she saw even more dismay on James's face. "Goodness, I'm honored," she said lightly. "And terrified. I suspect that at least a dozen local women want to do a war dance on my head."

"Well, that's the end of that," he said gruffly. "I'll move out. I was wrong to stay here in the first place."

Erica clenched her hands in her lap and fought to keep from making a sound of despair. "Hey, I don't mind what people say," she assured him. "You know, up in D.C., I'm used to Harold Brumby's calling me things like 'that big Amazon witch who stole my award.' I'm certainly not offended by rumors of being pregnant." She paused impishly. "Even by you."

James shook his head. "You've only been here a couple of weeks. I won't let gossip ruin your chances of making friends with people."

Echo stood up, and it was obvious from her tactful smile that she thought it best to leave. "I'll let you know how things go with my mysterious giant. 'Bye."

After Echo's station wagon disappeared down the driveway, Erica followed James into the house. Misery was a cold lump in her stomach.

"Hey, Wolfman, are you sure I'll be safe here alone, with violent turkeys flapping around at night?"

He slipped his feet into a pair of jogging shoes and began stuffing clothes into his leather tote. "You'll be fine, Red. I suspect that the Little People will look out for you. I'm sure they liked Dove, and you're her kin."

Erica laughed, and hoped that the sound was believable. *I need the Big People—one in particular.* "Where will you go?"

"To one of the motels on the strip."

"Hmmm. Addicted to lime-green furniture now, are you?"

"Yeah." He chuckled but kept his gaze fixed on the tote bag.

Erica shut her eyes for a moment, then quoted to herself: "Let him be sorrowing as he goes along, and not for one night alone. Let him become an aimless wanderer, whose trail may never be followed. His eyes have come to fasten themselves on one alone."

"There's a draft in here," James said abruptly. Frowning, he looked around.

Erica gazed at the goose bumps on his arms and hoped that he'd just been zapped by her lovespell. There was something else in the formula, something about wiping your spit on the intended. What the heck.

"You've got a spot of dirt on your arm," she told him. Erica licked her fingertips and dabbed quickly. "There."

He looked at her quizzically for several long seconds, then said, "Thank you, Erica Alice."

She pulled an imaginary skirt out from her jeans and curtsied. "Come back any time. I have lots of spit." Erica wanted to die at what her mouth had just said. *I have lots of spit*? No wonder he didn't find her sexy.

Oh, Lord, she was going to embarrass him horribly if she didn't get herself under control. Erica looked at her watch. "Yikes! I've gotta go! Lock the door when you leave, okay? I need to go to the grocery store before it closes. If I'm fixing dinner alone I, well, I . . ."

Alone. What a bad choice of words. It got trapped in her throat and wouldn't let much else out. "See ya around," she croaked, then patted his shoulder and fled out the door.

He caught her by one arm before she reached the porch steps. Erica trembled violently under his touch and tried not to look too desperate. He turned her to face him, and there was so much concern in his face that she didn't know how to react.

Her eyes knew, however, and they let big tears slip out. "Oh, hell," she muttered, and her voice added to the trouble by sounding miserable.

He took her by both shoulders, his hands gentle and ultimately even more destructive to her control. "Erica," he whispered, "Don't."

"Hey, it's only that I've gotten used to having company," she assured him. "If you leave, I'll have to buy a dog."

"I'll be just a few miles away. There's so much you still need to see and do. Don't worry, I won't desert you."

"I know. Sure." Erica smiled widely, using muscles

that would never recover from the strain, she figured. "You've been great. Thanks for giving me a chance to fit in."

He started to speak, seemed to have trouble, waited another second, then said finally, "I know you can fit in, but I also know that you can't stay."

Erica nodded. She had a successful business in Washington, and what kind of work could she possibly do here full time? But she wanted desperately to tell him that she'd gladly earn a million frequent-flyer points shuttling between her world and his, if he'd only ask.

She said in a playful, tear-soaked voice, "But I'm going to keep our bargain, Wolfman, and then I'll always have Dove's place if I want to visit."

He nodded. "I hope you do that."

That was it. She couldn't talk to him for another second without losing her dignity. Erica nodded jerkily. "Bye." She thought her voice did a great imitation of a laryngitis victim's. "The *kamama egwa* says see you later. *Do-na-da-go-huh.*"

"*Do-na-da-go-huh,*" he murmured, his eyes so still and dark that she could see herself in their reflection.

Erica stepped out of his grasp and went inside. As soon as she shut the door she pressed both hands to her mouth and walked quickly to the back room.

She sat on her rented bed and listened just long enough to hear James open and shut the door to Grandpa Sam's truck. Then she burrowed her face into the pillow on the bed and covered her ears, not caring that the last time she'd done anything so childlike, she'd been a child. She couldn't bear to hear him drive away.

The pillow was a kind listener for her sobs of defeat. She felt old and alone and hopeless; she'd expected to find someone, someday, and fall in love, but how in the world could she do that now that she wanted James Tall Wolf with single-minded devotion?

Erica knew she'd be sore from crying so hard, but

she cried anyway, her knees drawn up, her breath coming in big gulps that obliterated all outside sound.

So by the time she realized that there were noises in the house, James was already halfway across the bedroom to her. Erica bolted upright and covered her face. "No!" she wailed in humiliation.

"I can't take this anymore!" he shouted fiercely, grabbing her by both arms and pulling her off the bed.

Erica gasped for breath and ducked her face away. "I didn't m-mean for you to hear."

"I don't care what might happen later! I can't stand seeing you like this and I can't stand myself like this! Do you want me, Red? Do you want me to stay here? Do you want me to be your lover until you go back to Washington?"

She looked up at him in stark amazement. "W-what?"

"Oh, Red," he said hoarsely, and grasped her face between his big hands. "Look what I did to you. I'm sorry, Red."

"I d-don't need a m-mercy—"

"I'm the one who needs mercy, because I'm half out of my mind from wanting you." He pulled her closer and searched her eyes. "No promises, no regrets. Just you and me. You need a teacher, and I promise you that I'll be the best." His voice dropped to a graveled whisper, and he repeated, "Do you want me to be your lover?"

Dreams came true, magic was real, and for the first time in her life she belonged.

"Oh, *yes.*"


Darkness was a gentle cloak around the house, and the open windows let in just enough air to stir the flames on the big candles James had placed on the bedside stand.

Erica smoothed trembling hands over her hair and robe as she stood there in the flickering brightness watching him light more candles on the dresser. Her skin felt deliciously warm and receptive, as though the bath she'd just finished had cleaned away old sorrows.

James glanced up and saw her in the doorway. He straightened slowly, smiling at the way she eyed the white towel wrapped around his hips.

"Have a nice soak?" he asked. "You were only gone five minutes."

"I was lonely." Her heart beat a thready rhythm as she watched the candlelight dance on his body, polishing his skin to burnished copper.

He held out a hand. "That's the last bath you'll take alone here."

Somehow she made her rubbery legs cross the floor to him. Erica slipped her hands into his and smiled from the inside out, emotion rushing through her. "You made the room look beautiful," she murmured. "Even the furniture."

She watched his breath quicken as he looked down at her. Knowing that he wanted her, that he found her extremely desirable, gave Erica a confidence she'd never had before. "Let's go take a bath together," she told him.

He chuckled. "Easy, Red, easy. This is a very special occasion, and everything has to be done just so. That's why I wanted to wait until nighttime. Important ceremonies should be performed slowly and at night."

Erica realized that she was squeezing his big, warm hands and that his fingertips were making suggestive movements against her palms. "It's going to be a ceremony?" she murmured with a crooked smile. "Will I have to make a speech?"

He cradled her hands against the center of his chest. His dark eyes glittered with amusement and unmistakable anticipation. "No speech, but you'll probably want to say a few words in appreciation."

"Oh? Will I get some sort of award?"

He smiled wickedly. "You might call it that."

Erica placed her hands flat on his chest and smoothed them slowly over his sleek skin. "I've never touched a man this way before," she murmured, her face flushed more from excitement than uncertainty.

He inhaled sharply as she brushed her fingertips over him. "You missed out on a lot of awards, then, 'cause you're great at it."

Erica grasped his shoulders and looked up at him wistfully. "I read how-to books for fun. Ask me any clinical question. Go ahead. I know exactly how things are supposed to be done."

He put his hands on her waist and pulled her closer, until their torsos were almost touching. "Reading about it is like trying to learn football by correspondence course. Can't be done. You've got to get out there and really play."

"Make passes," she added, nodding sagely.

He winked at her. "And complete them."

"Without fumbling."

"Or rushing."

Erica slipped her arms around his neck. "And certainly without roughing the passer."

"Never." He gripped her sides and slid his hands down her hips. "But it's important to take possession any way you can."

Her voice throaty, Erica murmured, "Intercepting the pass is one way." She lifted her mouth to brush his.

James gripped her rump hard and teased her lips with quick, flirtatious kisses. "I like your offense."

"I like your defense."

"It's not working very well," he said huskily, and lifted her slightly, so that their mouths could merge.

The gentle invasion of his tongue made her moan and press upward for more. She quickly found herself exploring his mouth while he kept still, enjoying it.

"That's a very unusual defense you've got," Erica whispered.

"It's all part of a winning game plan," he said with a soft growl, then nibbled her lower lip.

Erica arched against him. Her spine felt loose and pliable; she could bend with him, wrap herself around him, easily become a part of him. "James. Oh, James. This was worth waiting thirty-three years for."

He stepped back, holding her gently by the shoulders as he studied her with quiet determination. "That's the way I hope you'll feel tomorrow morning too."

"You made me wait all afternoon," she said teasingly. "Now you're telling me I'll have to wait until morning?"

He jerked her to him with playful roughness. "You've got a smart mouth, doll."

Erica tilted her head back and inhaled the blended scent of masculine and feminine arousal. This was an essence no book could capture, no fantasy imagine. She looked at James through heavy, half-shut eyes. "It's actually a very uneducated mouth. Waiting for you to train it."

"*Erica*," he said in a helpless, rebuking tone, and kissed her so deeply that her knees buckled a little and she clutched his arms for support. Then he wound a hand into her hair and turned her head to one side. His lips brushing her ear, he murmured the details of his training techniques and how he hoped she would respond.

Leaning against him in perfect relaxation, her senses tuned to every nuance of his voice and scent and touch, she floated in a blissfully hypnotized state. When he stepped back and took her hands again, she gazed at him in speechless surrender.

"In the old days you and I probably would have done this at one of the village dances," he told her.

"The Cherokees must have had *great* dances."

James chuckled softly. "A lot of them were bawdy, by white standards. Some of them were downright shocking. But back then we thought that good old horniness was nothing to be embarrassed about."

"I'm not embarrassed," she assured him.

He grinned. "Neither am I. Let's dance." He placed her hands on his shoulders and put his on her waist. "Just stand still. The movement really wasn't much but a shuffling trot." He arched one brow. "And I don't feel like trotting at the moment."

Erica laughed. "Would we do this alone or in a group?"

"In a group, with the women in a line facing the men. There'd be a drummer to keep the beat and a leader to direct the songs."

"We'd have to dance, sing, and be shocking? It must have taken lots of practice."

"Practicing must have been half the fun." He pulled her hands away from his shoulders and placed them against his hands, palm to palm. "In the friendship dance, the two lines would circle, and the couples would touch each other according to the dance leader's hints."

He stroked her on the chin. "What I do, you do back."

"Ah. I've seen this sort of thing on *American Bandstand*." Her teasing mood faded, and she gently ran her hand along the strong line of his jaw.

He touched the tip of her nose; she touched back. He drew a path from one shoulder to another, running his finger over her robe; she did the same, and was very thankful that he wore no robe.

James cupped her shoulders and smoothed his hands down her back. Erica particularly enjoyed returning that gesture. Finally James stroked her arms; she caressed his far more intimately.

"You're cheating a little," he warned, but his slitted eyes gleamed with pleasure. James turned her to one side and stepped close to her. They shared an expectant look. "After the dance went on like that for a while, things got more serious," he murmured in a low, provocative tone.

"More serious?"

"The two lines got close, like this." He sidled up to her so that his thigh and hip were angled against hers. "For privacy." He chuckled with comic lechery. "You know what you can get away with in a crowd?"

"Show me," she whispered.

James stroked a finger down the soft white cotton of

her robe, then slid his hand under the lapel and cupped one of her breasts. The feel of his big, gentle hand on her, his thumb moving back and forth over her nipple, made her sway and utter a soft sound of need.

He put his arm around her waist and held her close while he touched the other breast. "At this point I'm sure I would have carried you off to the woods."

She pressed forward so that her breast filled his hand even more. "I would have carried *you*."

James moved his hand downward, unfastening the loosely tied belt of the robe. The garment parted all the way to her knees, and Erica thought nothing could feel so sensual as James's warm hand and the cool rush of air on the center of her body.

"Now I'd touch you lower," he whispered, as his fingertips trailed over her navel. Slowly he slid his hand into the hair between her thighs, and then he cradled her in his palm.

Erica moaned out loud and, quivering, bent her forehead against his shoulder. "Did the women touch the men?" she asked breathlessly.

His voice was a low rumble. "I was hoping you'd ask."

She flattened her hand over his stomach, watching the small, hard muscles tremble under her fingertips. His belly contracted as she tucked her fingers under the towel.

"I suspect this loincloth is going to fall off," she murmured, her hand wedged between soft cotton and rock-hard male abdomen.

He whispered in her ear, "In my version of the dance, the loincloth falls off."

And it did, quite gracefully, giving her a view of him that made all that had gone before seem tame. Her hand shook as she moved it lower, touching, exploring, reveling in the monumental differences between his body and hers.

"Is there a right way and a wrong way?"

Again he whispered in her ear. "Touch me as gently as you'd touch yourself, and I'll love it."

That seemed simple enough, and when the results made him quiver she knew she'd learned the lesson well. "You have a pulse there," she murmured in surprise.

He nestled his fingers deeper into her soft folds, and Erica forgot about everything but the sensations radiating outward from his touch.

"You have a nice pulse yourself," he replied. "And I know how to make it beat even faster."

He led her to the bed and stood looking at her, his dark eyes burning with affection and desire. "Take off your robe for me, Erica Alice."

Erica pushed the soft material from her shoulders and let it fall to the floor. Feeling a little shy, she studied his reaction stoically. "All six feet of me is happy you like tall women."

His gaze roamed down her body with uninhibited admiration. "So you thought you weren't sexy to me?"

"Yes. Skinny. Plain. Average. That's my self-image. Actually, I didn't think too much about the way I looked, until I met you. Then I wanted to be beautiful."

Trying to put her at ease, he gestured grandly toward his arousal. "Does this look like you're not beautiful to me? I have this reaction every time I get near you."

Erica stepped closer and caressed him. He made a throaty sound and roughly pulled her against him. She caught her breath as her belly cushioned the hard ridge of his body and her nipples touched his chest. Sliding her hands over his lean hips and thighs, Erica explored his taut contours.

Happiness burst inside her. "I'll never forget this night."

"I'll make sure of it," he whispered, and kissed her.

Erica put her arms around him and reveled in the power and possession of his embrace. The erotic sounds of their kiss were enough to make her body open with silky anticipation.

James drew her down on the shadowy bed and lay on his back with her half on top of him. Erica rubbed her thigh over his, feeling deliciously astonished at each new experience.

James molded one hand to her hip and seared a trail of sensation down the back of her leg, his fingertips brushing her intimately in passing. Erica realized that both she and he were panting lightly.

No fantasy could do justice to this, either—this breathless delight in sharing pleasure, this knowledge that they were partners even though he had so much experience and she had so little.

Erica cupped his face in the golden candlelight. "You are an incredible teacher." She spoke slowly, her voice husky. *And I love you,* she added silently.

He gave her a slight smile and inhaled sharply as she stroked his stomach. "Keep doing that and you'll graduate with honors."

A minute later he switched their positions, so that she lay looking up at him. Erica trembled as he brushed the back of his fingers down her torso, stroking her breasts and belly with long, slow movements.

She burrowed her face against his shoulder and kissed the hot, smooth skin. After a hesitant second she licked it with the tip of her tongue.

"More," he urged gruffly. "Don't hold anything back."

*As if I could resist you,* she thought. Erica tried to laugh, but the sound was more like a primitive begging for his touch. When he caressed her thighs her hips rose instinctively. Deep in a still-reasoning corner of her mind she was intrigued by the basic forces that had taken hold of her.

"This is the most natural thing in the world," she told him, startled. "I don't even have to think about what to do."

James made a strangled sound, and she looked up to find his face ruddy with passion and amusement. "That's the way it's supposed to be. You learn quickly."

Against her hip his aroused body was wonderfully

mobile and eager. He prodded her gently, and the slow flexing of his hips brought explicit images to her mind.

He searched her half-shut eyes and saw the images there. "That's right," he murmured in a wicked, growling voice. "That's what I wanted you to think about."

Her back arched as his hand dipped between her thighs. "I feel so heavy and relaxed and *ripe*," she whispered in awe.

James drew the hand up, circled one of her breasts, and squeezed it sensually as his mouth covered the nipple. White-hot desire shot through her body, and Erica speared her fingers into his hair.

He tantalized her as if she were a rich fruit he wanted to take whole into his mouth. The uninhibited loving left her breasts wet from his lips and tongue.

Erica made a high-pitched keening sound. She was lost in a haze of pleasure; nothing had ever felt so good in her whole life. She could have died happy, feeling James's lips on her this way.

He whispered earthy compliments against her skin during those brief moments when his tongue wasn't involved otherwise. They were the crude kind of words Erica heard construction workers bandy when good-looking women walked by a work site. If the workers had ever used such language about her, they'd been careful to make sure she didn't hear.

"Oh, thank you," she told James in rapt gratitude. "I needed that."

He lifted his head to smile at her, and the half-wild look of arousal in his expression excited her even more. He kissed her. "Later I want you to talk to me that way."

"Now," she said eagerly.

James chuckled deep in his chest and put a hand over her mouth. "It wouldn't be a good idea."

She knew her eyes must have looked huge with understanding, because he chuckled again. "Later, Red," he murmured. "Your voice is too sexy."

He moved down her body, kissing, nibbling, sucking

her skin roughly. Erica forgot about talking when James coaxed her legs apart and grasped her gently. "Easy, now," he murmured in a soothing way, as his fingers became part of her.

With a ragged gasp of pleasure she pushed against his hand, aching for release. His mouth sank onto her, and he groaned happily at the taste and feel of her readiness. Erica lost all control and tugged at his hair, urging him to come to her and make this magnificent ceremony complete.

He whispered against her swollen flesh, "That's it, Red. Want me as much as I want you."

Half-crying with the fervor of emotion and sensation, she grasped the item he'd arranged on the bedside stand. It lay on top of its package, waiting grandly. Erica thought no other man in the world would have gone to so much trouble to make her feel safe and uninhibited at the same time.

She was beyond words; the best she could do was a hoarse mewling sound as she stroked the offering against his shoulder. He felt the odd texture against his skin and looked up, his eyes gleaming.

"Yeees?" he asked, his voice a coy rasp. But when he saw the look on her face he quickly knelt beside her and cupped his hand under her shoulders.

He pulled her upwards and watched as she prepared him with shaking hands. "Are you afraid?" he asked hoarsely, stroking the disheveled hair back from her forehead. "It won't hurt. I swear I won't let it hurt."

Devotion surged through her as she looked up at him. "Not afraid," she whispered raggedly. "I want you so much that I don't care if it hurts."

"Oh, Red." He put his hands on her shoulders and eased her back. Gently he caressed her face as he lowered himself on top of her.

"Like this?" she asked as she gripped him with her thighs.

"Perfect," he said, and it sounded like an understatement.

Their eyes met and held. Erica was lost in so many new experiences—the feel of his body nudging her patiently, the weight of him pushing her down into the mattress, the almost fierce look of controlled desire in his face.

The air seemed to hum with intensity, as if it might shatter into crystal fragments just from the swift harmony of their breaths.

Erica lifted her head and kissed him. "No more old maid, please." Then she added in a voice too sensual for him to resist, "Do it quickly, James."

He bowed his head to her shoulder and thrust into her with one smooth, sure movement that filled her completely. She felt her body stretching to accommodate him, but there was only that tightness, no pain.

Erica smiled, and tears came to her eyes. He drew back and looked at her anxiously. As her hips began to move in slow, erotic circles, he sighed with relief.

"No more volcano candidate," he murmured tenderly.

She shook her head, and somewhere in the midst of it she realized that the ache inside her was exploding. Erica shut her eyes and whimpered.

He felt the gathering of sensation and moved carefully, bending his head close to hers so that he could whisper delicious promises in her ear; promises of slower times, of many times, of all night and everything she ever wanted from a man.

Erica slid her feet over the backs of his thighs and rose wildly, her hands digging into his shoulders, her lips moving soundlessly against his jaw.

Caught in her abandoned writhing, he moaned her name and, trembling violently, managed to thrust only once more before he joined her in a trance of sensation.

They rode the cloud down together, looking into each other's eyes, hands moving in gratitude over damp, hot skin, mouths meeting to promise more.

Erica made herself admit that he didn't think of this as anything serious, that he wanted her out of friendship and desire, not love. But she knew also that they had given each other something special, and there would always be a bond between them because of it.

The candlelight made yellow flecks in his eyes, like golden stars gleaming in a night sky. "*Da-nitaka*," he murmured.

Erica stroked a fingertip along his cheekbone and asked tenderly, "What does it mean, Wolfman?"

"They are together." He put his arms under her and lifted her slightly. Erica was lost in his gaze.

James arched gently inside her. "Their spirits are so close that they share one body," he explained. "*Da-ni-taka*."

Forever, she added silently. Some day she hoped he'd want that too.

# *Eight*

Erica quickly discovered that James had a marvelous way of turning everything into foreplay or afterplay.

Such as at that moment. He sincerely wanted to know about her construction company, but he had his head pillowed on her naked rump and he kept dawdling a finger down her spine.

"Why'd you decide to study civil engineering in college?"

Erica hugged a pillow under her chin and tried to think despite the fact that he was nibbling her right hip. "I was good in math and science, and I thought I'd make the world a better place by learning to build highways. After I graduated I decided that the last thing the world needed was more strips of concrete covered with oil slicks and flat animals."

Now he politely kissed the spot he'd bitten. "So where'd you learn about building houses?"

"When I was at school I worked summers for a residential contractor, a woman. She wanted to give women a chance in the business, and half her crew was female. You wouldn't believe the looks we'd get when we'd show up at a construction site with our tool belts and hard hats. We had T-shirts printed up that said, 'Yes, we've heard the one about the lady carpenter.' "

"So that's where you learned to use a drill," he said ruefully, and began nuzzling the small of her back.

Erica chuckled, and slumped lazily onto the pillow. His nuzzling destroyed coherent thought. Finally she twisted around and grabbed his bad knee. "Poor baby," she said in a crooning voice, and began kissing the surgical scars that framed the kneecap.

"Sympathy. Ah. Hmmm."

She placed kisses up his leg and scrutinized several tiny white dots on the top of his thigh. "I'd thought that these were just reverse freckles. But they're scars."

He cleared his throat and said softly, "That's where I used to give myself steroid injections. But mostly I put them here." James slapped his rump. "Hurt like hell."

Erica rested her cheek against the scars on his thigh and curled one hand protectively over his leg. "Was it worth it?"

His voice was gruff. "At the time, yes. But I'll never let a kid of mine do it."

"How do steroids help a player, besides making him bigger and stronger?"

"They make you so aggressive that you want to rip people apart. That's a good attitude for football; not so good for anything else. The last season I played, I tore up my locker before every game. Pulled it off the wall and beat the hell out of it. And I wasn't the only player doing crazy things like that."

"Oh, James." She stroked his leg tenderly. "Is that why you didn't come home very often? Because you were so messed up while you played ball?"

"Yes." He ran his hand over her hair, caressed it back from her face, then sank his fingers into it as if the texture were comforting. "I wasn't a good person to be around. The money and the fame didn't change me, but when my knee started to give me problems and I took steroids to compensate, I turned into a real touchy SOB. At least I recognized the change. So I stayed away from my family as much as I could."

After a second, he added, "And there was another reason. Travis's wife."

Erica listened in stunned silence as he told her about times when Danna Tall Wolf had tried to corner him, and the Christmas eve she'd slipped into his old bedroom while Travis slept in the room across the hall. James had firmly set her out and locked his bedroom door.

"That was the last time I came home for a holiday," he said.

"Does Travis know any of this?"

"No. And he never will. He can think what he wants to about me. I won't hurt him with the truth about Danna."

"Thank you for sharing that with me."

James turned her face toward him and cupped her chin. "I trust you with it."

Between kisses she asked softly, "What are you going to do when you move down to the reservation for good? I mean, what kind of business?"

"I'm going to build furniture. Custom pieces. I've already sold a few things to friends."

"That's great, James." She grasped one of his brawny hands and studied the callouses. "Yep. You have the hands to be a builder."

"That's not wood stain, that's my skin color."

"Strong, tough hands, but not clumsy." Erica gave him a solemn look. "Though you do have knuckles like a gorilla."

James tugged his hand away and tweaked her nipple. "I've played football since I was five. Plus my father ran a logging business, and we boys spent all our spare time cutting timber. These hands have been through a lot."

He wasn't angry, but she raised his hands and nuzzled them in apology, anyway. "I know, Wolfman, I know. I think they're wonderful hands. Very sexy."

That made his eyes gleam. "They look good against your skin."

"Hmmm. Show me." Grinning, she stretched out and put her head on his stomach.

"A lap cat. That's what you are."

"What's 'cat' in Cherokee?"

*"Wis-sah."* James walked his fingers down her belly. "Here, *wis-sah*, here, *wis-sah* . . ."

They both jumped a little as they heard a car coming up the driveway. They'd been alone for two days, and naked virtually all of that time. The outside world had ceased to exist.

James got up quickly and dressed in jeans and a T-shirt. He parted a window curtain and glanced out. "Lancaster. Alone."

Erica hopped out of bed and grabbed her clothes. She didn't know what James might say or do in Echo's defense.

By the time she went outside James and Drake Lancaster were standing in the yard, embroiled in a tense discussion. James had his arms crossed over his chest, and Lancaster lounged against a muddy, dented pickup truck. Both he and the truck looked as if they'd been through hell.

Drake's dark, frowning gaze swiveled gratefully toward Erica as she stopped beside James. "Do you know where Echo is?" Drake asked, his voice gruff.

"No." Erica couldn't decide what to think about this bewildering man, but she did know that Echo seemed to be the kind of woman who loved carefully and for good reason. "What's wrong?"

"I have to leave. I don't have time to say good-bye, and there are things she doesn't understand, that she's worried about—"

"We know," James interjected grimly.

"I love her. There's no other woman. My work is unusual, but it's not illegal. Or immoral. At least not by most people's standards."

*By most people's standards?* Erica gazed at Drake Lancaster quizzically, and was touched by the quiet brand of anguish in his eyes. "We'll tell her what you said," she assured him. "James?"

James glanced at her, saw her beseeching gaze, and sighed. "All right."

Drake reached into a shirt pocket. "Erica, you need to take care of this. I know you have one similar to it." He held out a familiar-looking good medallion. "It belongs to Tess."

Erica gasped and took the medallion from him. "What are you doing with it?"

"I promised her that I'd have it translated. Can you do that for me? I'll send for it later."

Erica gaped at him in utter astonishment. "What's going on with Tess? Is she all right?"

"Your cousin is fine. She's on her way out of the country. There was a misunderstanding about a diamond she owned. She was in trouble. It wasn't her fault, but she's under protection now."

James took the medallion and looked at Drake carefully. "You had her hidden up in the caves near Bryson."

Drake nodded. "I wasn't in charge; a friend of mine was. She's under his protection. There's no need to worry about her." He gazed at Erica in apology. "I promise that all of this will be explained to you eventually."

"What about my sister?" James asked with quiet authority.

"I'll be back."

"When?" Erica asked.

"I don't know. Tell her to wait. Tell her . . ." He paused, searching for words, a private man who didn't feel comfortable discussing his emotions. "Tell her this is just the beginning for us."

"All right," Erica said softly.

"Good-bye." He shook hands with her, then held out a hand to James. "Trust me. I'm on the level."

After a second James returned the shake. "If you're not, don't ever let me catch you inside the Qualla boundary again."

"Good enough," Drake agreed pleasantly. He went to his truck and climbed inside. "Oh. For your information, Erica, your great-great-grandparents are buried in California, near San Francisco. Tess found their graves.

"They lived there until sometime in the eighteen-fifties. They started a big vineyard and named it Glen Mary, after a daughter who died when she was still a baby. Tess never learned where Justis and Katherine went after they left California, but they eventually came back there to die. They're buried next to their daughter."

"Thank you," Erica said numbly, stunned.

She and James watched Drake Lancaster drive away. Erica took her cousin's medallion and stared at it in consternation. "Mystery," she said plaintively. "More mystery. What now?"

James grasped her hand and led her back inside. "When in doubt, get naked and do the friendship dance."

James came to a disturbing realization: He'd never been happier. The more he learned about Erica, the more there was to know. They shared many interests, and her fascination with the Cherokee language and lore was inexhaustible, much like her fascination with making love.

He tried not to wonder if that fascination had little to do with him personally, and he kept reminding himself that she was an eager listener when he talked about his plans for creating a co-op where local furniture craftsmen could design and sell their work.

After a week of enjoying each other, they took the medallions to show to Grandpa Sam.

Becky had a date, but on her way out she presented Erica with a pair of beautiful deerskin ankle boots she'd made. They had elaborate beadwork across the toes.

In the shape of big butterflies.

"For bringing my brother back home," Becky announced.

James's heart sank at the guarded way Erica smiled, and he wondered what she was thinking.

But she laughed at the butterflies and seemed mesmerized by the workmanship in the boots. "Why don't you make these to sell?" she asked Becky.

"Aw, it's just a hobby. The restaurant keeps me busy."

"If you ever want to market them, I'd be glad to help. I have a friend who works for Neiman-Marcus. I could show these to him."

Becky looked pleased, but James only thought, When you go back to D.C.

After Becky left, Erica changed her tennis shoes for the boots and padded proudly around the Tall Wolf kitchen. Grandpa Sam, seated at the kitchen table rolling bean dumplings, chortled at her.

"You got Cherokee feet now," he proclaimed.

James went to Echo, who stood at the stove, and put his arm around her. "Have you heard from Drake?"

Echo stirred a pot of thick stew and shook her head. "But he'll be back."

"No man can resist a woman of the wolf clan," James teased gently. "And I think Lancaster's trustworthy."

Erica came over and patted her arm. "I agree."

Echo gave them both a meaningful look, then smiled up at her brother. "You've mellowed since you came home this time. I wonder why?"

James glanced over her head and met Erica's eyes. She winked at him as if his sister's innuendo were a cute joke. He winced inwardly. Now was as good a time as any to break the news "I'm here to stay this time."

"James!" Echo dropped the spoon and hugged him. Erica gave him a smile that cut him to the heart. She wasn't upset about his announcement, that was certain.

Sam trotted over and threw his arms around both of his grandchildren. Then he grabbed Erica and hugged her. "I knew the first night I saw you that you were

good for James! I said to the girls, 'That's the one!
That's the one he's been waitin' for.' "

"Grandpa, Erica and I are just friends," James
interjected quickly, trying to keep her from feeling more
uncomfortable.

She shot him a strained look but made a joke; she
didn't want anyone to make permanent plans for the
two of them, that was obvious.

Echo, sensing the tension, shooed Grandpa to the
table with Erica in tow, ordering them both to finish
the dumplings. In Erica's honor, dinner was to be
old-time Cherokee fare—dumplings made from brown
beans and cornmeal, squirrel stew, baked cucumbers
and sweet-potato cakes.

James made some vague excuse about going up-
stairs to get the box of Civil War memorabilia left by
his great-great-grandfather William. At the top of the
stairs he sat down and lit a cigar, but held it limply in
his hands and sat frowning into space.

He couldn't call off his bargain with Erica; that
wouldn't be fair. But if they had no future together
how could he go on like this for another five weeks,
needing her more each day, living so close to her
thoughts and feelings that he was *da-nitaka* with her,
standing in her soul?

Well, there was only one way to help this situation—
spend as little time with her as possible until she went
home. James got to his feet and moved wearily down
the hallway, missing her already.

From the corner of his eye he caught sight of a
photograph, and stopped to study it. The beautiful
smiling brunette was Danna, Travis's dead wife. James
could barely stomach the sight of her even now.

She'd taken malicious pleasure in skewering him
after he offered her the house in Chicago. She'd come
home and told Travis that his brother had asked her to
be his mistress.

Travis hadn't believed that nonsense, but he'd been

furious about James's intervention in his marriage. And thus the bitterness had begun between them.

James continued down the hall, his teeth gritted. Erica was no Danna—he hated even thinking Erica's name so soon after looking at Danna's photograph. No, she wouldn't ruin him the way Danna had ruined Travis.

Erica would ruin him through decency, kindness, and her honest need for a temporary teacher and companion. Erica would ruin him because he knew that falling in love with her was right, and good, and hopeless.

It was hard to concentrate on history after James's disgruntled reaction to his family's matchmaking comments. Erica kept hearing his grim voice saying that he and she were just friends. He certainly wanted *that* point made clear.

She faked her appetite during dinner, and was glad when they adjourned to a card table Echo had set up in the den. Erica sat stiffly in a folding chair and watched Grandpa Sam spread out photocopied letters, photographs, Confederate money, and other memorabilia.

"Got a present for you, Eh-lee-ga." Sam picked out a tinted contemporary portrait and handed it to her. "Guess that was made sometime around the big war."

"World War II," James explained.

Erica gazed at a studio portrait of a mature, attractive Cherokee woman wearing a black dress with big white lapels. A fat braid of graying black hair wound around her head like a crown, and there was enough imperial strength in her eyes to make the crown seem appropriate.

Her eyes. Gallatin green eyes. Erica gasped softly. "Is this Dove?"

Grandpa Sam grinned. "Yep. She gave me that a few years ago. Said she wanted to tell folks that a good-looking man was carrying her picture around."

Erica felt James's fingertips on her chin. "Gimme a look, Red," he murmured gruffly. He held the photo beside her face and studied the similarity in eye color. "I wonder if the green eyes started with old Justis Gallatin?"

"They must have, because I'm not directly related to Dove. My cousin Kat is." She glanced at Sam. "Thank you. This picture means a lot to me."

"Dove was a good friend," he answered solemnly. "But you know, there was a lot of mystery about her. She didn't come here until after the war. Never would talk about the years before, but I think she must have had a husband, maybe even some children. Don't know what happened to 'em."

James handed the two medallions to him. "Can you make sense of these, Grandpa?"

Sam hummed and squinted as he ran one knotty, olive-brown finger under the symbols. "This is old style—different ways of saying things, words I don't recognize. Tribe has more than one way of talking. Oklahoma way, North Carolina way. Back before the removal, there were even more ways."

"Different dialects," Becky explained.

"Can you make out anything?" Erica asked anxiously.

Sam pointed to one side of Tess's medallion. "Katlanicha Blue Song, daughter of Jesse and Mary Blue Song, sister of Anna, Elizabeth, and Sallie. Then . . . something about a place in Georgia, 1838."

"Katlanicha." Her heart racing, Erica looked at James.

"The journal," he said, nodding, his eyes black with fascination. "The woman on the trail of tears."

"Of the Blue clan." Erica pressed trembling hands together and tried not to squeal with delight. "That was my great-great-grandmother!"

"Blue clan," Echo murmured, smiling. "Good. Now you know your clan. That was the most important connection a Cherokee had."

"Still is," Sam said firmly. He studied her medallion.

"Can't make this one out much. Only thing I recognize is this." He pointed to a long row of symbols on one side. "The trail where they cried. That's the Cherokee word for the Trail of Tears. She was sent off with the rest of the tribe, I guess."

"But she obviously escaped from the man who kidnapped her," Erica said softly. James explained to Echo and Sam about the journal article.

"Let me keep these a while and I'll figure 'em out," Sam told her, looking at the medallions.

"Thank you, Grandpa Sam!"

"You're welcome, Eh-lee-ga of the Blue clan."

Erica was so proud that she forgot James's earlier coolness and grabbed his hand. He smiled pensively but bent over and kissed her fingers like an old-world gallant.

"Now I can call you Red Blue."

She laughed, and Echo pointed out, "In the old days you couldn't marry inside your own clan. Remember that. If you stick with tradition you have to marry a man from one of the others. Bird, Long Hair, Paint, Potato, Deer, or Wolf."

James let go of her hand and said drolly, "I think Erica needs to find someone from the Democrat clan."

"Independent," she corrected, smiling while his impersonal words knifed through her.

Erica tried to concentrate as Grandpa Sam began talking about James's great-great-grandfather. William Tall Wolf had joined a Cherokee infantry regiment during the Civil War.

William, the half-breed son of the first James Tall Wolf and Amanda, his Quaker wife, had apparently been a well-educated young man. Sam read from voluminous letters William had written home, letters filled with emotion and colorful details.

"William's regiment even caught itself a Cherokee Yankee," Grandpa Sam said proudly, thumping a letter. "Up in Tennessee. A half-breed, like William. But a

*Yankee* spy. William says here the fellow was about his own age. Maybe twenty-one, twenty-two."

Grandpa Sam fished around in the clutter on the table and picked up a tarnished locket. "That spy told William to take this to his wife and son up in New York. Wanted her to have it after the war."

"What happened to the spy?" Erica asked.

"They shot him."

"They shot one of their own tribe?"

"He was a Yankee spy. The way William wrote about him, he musta been a nice feller, and I guess they felt bad about shooting him, but it was wartime."

Erica took the locket and gently examined it. More than a century's passing couldn't keep her from feeling sorry for the young man who'd died. "Why didn't William take this to the spy's family?"

"Tried to, I reckon. Probably just couldn't find them after the war. People got so scattered."

Erica opened the badly aged locket and peered inside. "Hmmm. There's an inscription. It's almost worn off." She added wistfully, "Maybe the spy rubbed his fingers over it for good luck."

James took the locket and went to a lamp beside Grandpa Sam's recliner. He squinted at the engraving and read slowly, "There's part of a date—I can only make out the year. I think it's 1860. And there are initials. R.T.—I can't make out the third one—to E.A.R."

Erica gazed at him in shock. "E.A.R.?"

James nodded. "Ear."

She vaulted up and hurried to his side. "Let me see." Erica grasped the locket in quivering hands while James studied her with bewilderment. "Ear!"

"Ear," he repeated patiently.

Erica read and reread the initials in disbelief. "My great-grandmother's maiden name was Ear! I mean, her initials were E.A.R. It's always been a family joke. Erica Alfonza Rutherford. I'm named after her!"

With a yelp of excitement Echo joined them, staring

at the unimportant-looking little locket in awe. "What do you know about her?"

"Wait," James said, shaking his head. "Red, how could this be your great-grandmother? If she had a son, he'd be your grandfather. Your grandfather couldn't have been born during the Civil War. It'd make him too old."

Erica shook her head raggedly, still studying the locket. "Grandpa Gallatin was almost seventy when my father was born. He never had any children by his first three wives. One divorced him, and two died. His fourth wife—my grandmother—was a twenty-year-old actress."

"Get 'em as kittens, train 'em right," James offered wryly. "Good idea."

Erica punched his arm. "Grandpa Gallatin was a third-rate stage actor in New York and a first-rate lecherous old coot, or so my mother claims. My dad was born two days after his sixty-ninth birthday."

Echo patted her arm enthusiastically. "Then maybe this was your great-grandmother's locket! What do you know about your great-grandfather?"

"His first name was Ross—that's all I've ever been told. I know that he was half-Cherokee and had two brothers—and a sister who died as a baby." She handed the locket to James so that his steady hands could hold it under the light.

"R.T.," he repeated softly, looking at the first set of initials. "Could be that the last initial used to be a *G* for Gallatin."

Erica collapsed weakly into Grandpa Sam's recliner. "That would mean that my great-grandfather was shot by his own tribesmen for being a spy from the Union army."

"A Yankee," Grandpa Sam said in a tone of regret, as if that were the only sad part of it. "Oh, well."

Feeling very defeated, Erica murmured, "I'd hoped that he'd be an . . . Indian."

Echo nodded. "Traditional, you mean. A Cherokee, not a white man who happened to have Cherokee blood."

"Yes. I thought I'd feel closer to my Indian heritage once I knew more about him."

"Ross must have been a hero to the Union forces," James told her gently. He thought for a second, then snapped his fingers. "And if he was, then his name ought to be listed in the records at the National Archives."

Erica nodded. "Maybe I can check over the phone."

James's silence made her look at him closely. His expression was guarded. "I'll check for you. I'm going to be in Washington for the next two weeks."

Somehow she managed to hide the fact that she'd just been knocked down. Erica gave him a quizzical frown. "Oh? Business?"

He nodded. "If I'm moving back here, I have arrangements to make."

"I need to check in at my office, so I'll go—"

"Nope, you stay here and learn about life on the reservation. That was the deal."

Erica clutched the arms of her chair. Had he grown bored with her so soon? He'd hardly let her out of his sight for a week, and now, suddenly, he was anxious to leave. Had he simply done his duty in bed and then felt he could move on? "You agreed that I could take care of my business," she reminded him.

"Later. You can go to Washington after I come back."

So she'd be out of his way around Dove's house, Erica thought in despair. He'd realized that she was in love with him, and this trip was his way of reminding her not to take their arrangement too seriously.

"Okay. Sure," Erica told him affably, and shrugged. She was aware that Echo and Grandpa Sam were watching the scene with quiet interest.

The look she got from James was so intense that she knew he'd been concerned about her reaction to his trip. Erica kept her face composed. She wouldn't cry and act as if she were about to be abandoned; she wouldn't hang on to his coattails simply because he'd just given her the best week of her life.

If there was any way of winning him over, it certainly wasn't by acting possessive.

"You don't mind?" he asked.

"No. I've got plenty to keep me busy. Becky's going to teach me how to do beadwork."

"Beadwork, huh?"

The tone of his voice suggested that he didn't see how beadwork could fill up all her time, and the thought bothered him, somehow.

"And I'm going to get out and meet people," she added.

"People?"

"You know, those two-legged creatures who cause so much trouble."

"So you want trouble?"

She smiled jauntily. "Depends on what kind of people I meet."

"Be careful. The men around here are afraid of drills."

"I'll just have to figure out other ways of getting their attention."

He hooked a thumb in the waistband of his faded jeans and said lightly, "There are no elevators here."

Grandpa Sam, who looked confused by the conversation and exasperated by the change of subject, said, "Eh-lee-ga, you keep the locket. If you find out it's not your great-grandma's, give it back to me. Now y'all come sit down. I've got more letters to read."

Erica got up from the recliner, awkwardly trying not to touch James, who was standing in front of it, doing a good impression of an immovable object.

She couldn't avoid brushing against him. Erica raised her eyes and looked at his unfathomable expression, feeling miserable and hoping that it didn't show. She held out her hand for the locket.

He calmly put her family heirloom in his jeans pocket. "I might need to study it some more."

"I don't see why," she said just as the phone rang and Echo went into the kitchen to take the call.

"You be a good little girl," James said to Erica, "and I'll give it to you when I get back from Washington." He smiled, his arched brow conveying an innuendo that only she could see.

Erica's misery turned to quiet anger. He had that squint-eyed appearance of determination on his face, that smug masculine look he'd had after he'd trapped her in the elevator and after he'd tackled her in an alley.

"Maybe I won't want it anymore," she said pleasantly.

"Oh, you'll want—"

"Grandpa! James!" Echo ran into the den, her eyes frantic. "Travis's house trailer is on fire!"

# *Nine*

Thick, acrid smoke floated through the June night, and Erica's stomach recoiled as soon as she leaped from the back of Grandpa Sam's pickup truck. There was something particularly noxious about the burning scent of man-made building materials. The fake woods and space-age plastics that made up a modern house trailer tended to burn quickly and emit suffocating chemical fumes.

And James was already running toward the door of the trailer.

Erica raced after him, leaving Echo to grip Grandpa Sam's arm in an attempt to keep him from following James. One of the reservation's fire trucks was already on the scene, and Erica saw James grab a volunteer fire fighter by the sleeve of his overcoat.

She reached the two men in time to hear the volunteer yell something about Travis. James bolted inside the trailer.

The volunteer started after him, then glanced around and saw Erica heading full-tilt in the same direction. She dodged his outflung hands and leaped to the trailer steps two seconds after James had disappeared in a hell of black smoke.

Erica took one last breath of fresh air and vaulted into a roasting darkness that smelled like a coal furnace. She stumbled against furniture and pawed the air with both hands, as if she could clear a path in it.

No one could remain conscious more than a minute or two in that suffocating prison of smoke. Dear Lord, where were Travis and James?

Erica struggled forward blindly, the roar of nearby flames filling her ears, her lungs aching with the effort to find oxygen. She slammed into a wall, fell back against another, and realized that she was in some sort of hallway.

When she heard the sound of ragged coughing, she lunged forward and collided with someone. "James!"

"Get out of here!"

He was hunched forward, pulling Travis slowly along the floor. Erica anchored her hands under Travis's arm and threw herself backward. She and James were both coughing violently now.

"Get out!" he yelled again.

"Save your breath!"

They got Travis to the end of the hallway and angled him toward the outer door. Travis moved weakly, trying to help himself, and by then Erica was so light-headed that she was ready to crawl beside him.

When she fell down she felt James's big hand sink into her shirt. He was staggering, but he managed to jerk her back to her feet. Together they used their last few seconds of strength to drag Travis to the trailer door.

Suddenly the air wasn't quite so hot, and light shone through the smoke. Someone grabbed Erica and carried her outside. She lifted her head groggily and looked back to see other men pulling out James and Travis.

James was safe. Good. Now she could breathe again. It was time to pass out.


There was a whole pack of fidgeting Tall Wolves in the medical clinic of the reservation, and one lone butterfly of the Blue clan who wasn't allowed to sit up or even flutter a wing.

"Keep still," James ordered. He sat beside her on the gurney and held a cold compress to her forehead.

Erica eyed him in dismay. His face was haggard, his eyes were bloodshot, his golf shirt and jeans were filthy, and he had a red burn welt across one forearm. All she'd done was faint, and she felt fine by then, but he wouldn't let her get up.

"You're the one who needs to be lying here," she told him.

He bent over and kissed her—not for the first time since she'd come to, with her head in his lap—and then he whispered gently, "Keep still or I'll tie you down."

Travis was already sitting up on the gurney across the room, looking disgruntled because the doctor kept pressing a cold stethoscope to his bare chest. Echo and Grandpa Sam went from one gurney to another with the regularity of mother wolves checking their cubs.

Becky arrived, terrified because she'd heard vague details about a fire at Travis's place that involved injuries, and she made a round of the gurneys twice before she was satisfied enough to calm down.

"What happened?" she asked tearfully.

"I drove up and saw smoke coming out of the windows," Travis told her. "I radioed for help and then I went inside to save what I could."

Becky hugged him fiercely. "You dumb brother, you almost got killed. There's not anything worth that much."

Travis looked across the room and met James's eyes. "I wanted my pictures of Danna."

James nodded. "I would have gotten them for you if I could have."

Both men glanced away. Travis looked at Erica. "What you did was special. I'll never forget it."

Erica winced inwardly. He could compliment her, but not James. She watched the muscles tighten in James's jaw. He took her hand and occupied himself by stroking the back of it.

In the awkward silence that followed, Erica decided it was time to build more bridges, even at the risk of being a meddler. "Travis," she said softly. "James loves you very much, and I wish you'd say that you love him. This is a wonderful family; I envy you all. You don't know how lucky you are." She paused, fighting a knot of emotion in her throat.

"In my family everybody is too busy making career statements to notice one another. We never talk about our feelings." She looked at Grandpa Sam. "My mother put her parents in a nursing home before they needed to go." She looked from Becky to Echo. "My half sisters have always believed that being in the same family meant we had to compete with one another—at school, at our jobs, in terms of the clothes we wore, the number of men we had."

Erica smiled wryly. "I didn't fare very well in two out of those four areas." She looked into James's eyes and felt his hand close tightly around hers. "Nobody would do for me what you did for your brother tonight." Then she looked at Travis. "Nobody would get involved in my problems and try to help the way James tried to help you."

Grandpa Sam made a gruff noise and crossed his arms over his chest. "I'm an old man, and I might die any day," he said bluntly. "I want to know that my grandsons are at peace with each other."

Travis looked at James for a moment. Frowning, he got off the gurney, took his blackened uniform shirt, and started for the door. When he got there he stopped, turned around, and told James hoarsely, "I don't know if I can make peace with you, but I do love you."

"I love you too," James answered. "And I understand how you could love Danna so much that nothing else mattered."

The look on Travis's face told Erica that he had never expected to hear those words from James. Slowly his gaze slid thoughtfully to her, then after a moment returned to James.

"Welcome home, little brother," he murmured, then turned and left the room.

James awoke with a painful ache in his bad knee and a delicious ache in other areas. He had slept lightly, dreaming about the long bath he and Erica had taken together, the way she'd licked the burn mark on his arm, the way she'd risked drowning to do incredible things to him while he lay in the tub smiling helplessly.

Later, in bed, he'd curled on his side and snuggled her against his body, with her legs draped lazily over his hips. He put his mouth next to her ear and told her more of the ancient Cherokee stories, while he kept one hand moving patiently between her thighs.

When he finished, the praises she moaned with such breathless emotion had nothing to do with his story-telling ability.

What now? Could he bring himself to leave for Washington? *No.* He'd simply tell her the truth—that he loved her and hoped that she was willing to love him too. If she wanted to try, somehow they'd make the situation work even if they lived apart.

James sighed with anticipation and reached out to draw her to him. When he couldn't locate her he sat up quickly and looked around. Morning sunlight filtered through the living-room curtains; he heard birds singing outside, but the house was terribly silent.

James rolled to the edge of the bed and reached for his watch on the nightstand. He wasn't human until he knew the time, an old discipline from all the years when he'd had to get up early every morning for football practice. When he moved back to the reservation for good he intended to quit wearing a watch.

Under the timepiece was a slip of notebook paper. James squinted, then grabbed it and read the uncaring lines bitterly. "I've gone exploring for the day. Have a good flight to D.C. See you in two weeks. *Kamama egwa.*"

She didn't give a damn if he left.


The next afternoon, when Travis drove into the yard, Erica was sitting on the front porch grimly making herself absorb reality—the latest issue of *Forbes*, a week's worth of *Wall Street Journals*, and an issue of *Cosmopolitan* containing an article titled, "How to Survive when You're all Wrong for Mr. Right."

She'd spent the previous day in Asheville, shopping as if she were a crazed Yuppie and telling herself that she wasn't buying a whole new wardrobe just to entice James. She'd come back after dinner and spent the evening at the tribe's bingo hall. When she finally couldn't avoid it any longer she'd gone to Dove's empty house and sat on the front porch staring moodily at the mountains and stars.

As Travis got out of his patrol car she put down her stack of magazines and newspapers and went to greet him. He smiled at her wearily. Erica knew from talking to the sisters that he'd moved into the house with them and Grandpa Sam. The fire had destroyed everything he owned, and it would take time for the insurance money to come through.

"James asked me to make sure you stayed safe from turkeys," he told her. "Echo and Becky said you should come to dinner at the house every night." He chuckled. "Grandpa said you should go after James."

Erica managed a wry smile while she thought sadly, *That's the last thing James wants.* She took a deep breath and told Travis, "I choose the dinner option."


James always enjoyed a good, burned steak, and he was in the most elegant place in Washington to get an excellent steak cooked to a crisp. He should have been happy, but he kept brooding about Erica.

With any luck she'd taken his family up on the dinner offer. That way they could make sure she didn't have to eat by herself or with strangers—especially the wrong kind of strangers. Men.

James took a sip of bourbon and decided there was no way in hell he could enjoy his steak as long as Stephen and his latest big-chested brunette made eyes at each other over theirs.

"Does Stevie want some more horseradish sauce on his meat?" Miss Chest of the Year crooned, angling a piece of steak at Stephen's grinning mouth.

"Anywhere you want to put it," he crooned back, rakishly arching a thick blond brow.

This prelude to their private dessert was too much for James to take. He tossed his napkin on the table. "I'm calling it a night. I'll see you tomorrow at your office."

"My man, my man," Stephen said anxiously, eyeing the half-eaten piece of charcoal on James's plate. "What's wrong? Steak too rare?"

"I'm just tired. Got a lot of work ahead of me."

Stephen squeezed his date's bare shoulders. James didn't know what invisible army was holding up her shimmery blue bodice, but it was losing the battle.

"Honey," Stephen said in a drawl, gazing into her eyes with grand melancholy, "my partner's moving away and selling his half of the business to me. What am I gonna do?"

"Oooh, we'll find you a different kind of partner," she said through puckered raspberry-colored lips.

"Good night," James interjected quickly. He thought of Erica's quaint dignity and how unglamorous she had looked to him at first. Now he knew that he loved her dignity, and glamour didn't matter.

"Jim, boy, I've got some news that'll perk you up." Stephen looked like a jovial tomcat who'd just caught a bird. "That she-devil who kicked me lost a half-million-dollar deal, thanks to her little escapade with the carpenter ants. George Gibson was about to sign her for two houses, but when he saw the story on the news he backed out. You know old George. He's 'bout as sweet as Howard Cosell, and twice as opinionated."

James gazed at his partner in grim astonishment. Erica had never mentioned the lost deal. No wonder she'd found time to visit the reservation. She'd just had months of lucrative work pulled out from under her. And it was his fault, because she'd never have been on the news if he hadn't caught her in that alley.

He owed it to her to get that job back, even if it meant that she'd have to leave North Carolina sooner than planned. "Steve, old buddy," he said, glancing meaningfully at Miss Chest, "don't stay out too late. We're going to twist George Gibson's arm in the morning."

Erica was in the kitchen making construction estimates on a house for Travis when she heard a car door slam. Thinking that one of the Tall Wolfs had dropped by to visit, she kept working.

But when she heard the thump, ka-thump of someone hobbling up the porch steps she thought, *James! And he's hurt his knee again.*

Erica ran to the front door. Lord, had he really been gone only six days? She didn't care why he'd come back, she was just glad—

Kat Gallatin stood there, looking like a little Cherokee princess except for the fact that she wore baggy hiking shorts and a T-shirt that read "*WOW. Women Of Wrestling.*"

Above a pink Reebok her right ankle was wrapped in tape, and she held a crutch up as if she'd been about to rap on the door with it.

Kat took one look at Erica's startled expression, clasped her chest dramatically, and said, "Don't open your door so quickly! I've heard there are Indians around here!"

Erica gave a sputtering laugh and grabbed her arm. "Come in! What are you doing here? How did you get hurt?" As she guided her cousin to the couch she glanced out the window at Kat's car, a souped-up old Mustang with mag wheels. It was appropriate.

"I got squashed defending a guy from the audience!" Kat settled on the couch, flipped back her waist-length hair, and propped her foot on the end of her crutch. "I was wrestling a monster named Lady Savage over in South Carolina two nights ago, and I got thrown out of the ring—but it was planned, you dig?"

"But I landed in this guy's lap and he thought I was really hurt. So when Lady Savage comes after me, he gets between us, and she doesn't like men, 'cause her husband just ran off with her sister, so she *tries to kill this guy.*"

Erica stared at her cousin in amazement. "What did he do?"

"He wouldn't hit back! I guess he didn't want to hit a woman, even a big hulk like Lady Savage. So I had to punch her in the chops before she brained him, and she kicked me in the ankle!"

Kat sighed. "So now I have a fracture and I can't work for two months. I'd like to find that guy and twist his moustache off." She paused, looking pensive. "But he had a great moustache. And he tried to protect me."

"Oh, Kat. Do you need money?"

She shook her head. "No, I'm not broke yet. I heard from the lawyer that you were hanging out over here in Injun land, so I thought I'd drop by and okay my plan with you. I'm going back to Gold Ridge to camp on our property for a while. You know, back to nature, and all that."

"Of course I don't mind. And I'm sure Tess won't, either."

"I tried to call Tess, but she's vamoosed somewhere."

Erica explained what she knew about Tess's situation. When she finished Kat was wide-eyed.

"Nothing that exciting ever happens to me!"

"Somebody named Lady Savage throws you out of the ring and a spectator risks a beating to rescue you? That's not exciting?"

Kat laughed, and the two of them started a companionable conversation about all the things Erica had learned regarding her branch of the Gallatin family and Dove. Kat gave her the third medallion to show to Grandpa Sam, and by the time Kat left for Gold Ridge she had an armload of history books and was calling herself *Wis-sah*, for cat.

She roared away in the Mustang, spinning gravel, one small hand brandishing a rubber tomahawk out the window. She'd bought it at one of the tourist shops in Cherokee town.

Erica laughed in affectionate disbelief and wondered if Gold Ridge was ready for Wis-sah Gallatin.

One of the tribe's councilmen came to the door of the Tall Wolf house that night as everyone was finishing dinner. Travis looked surprised to see him, but made no comment about the visit. He introduced the man to Erica as Jack Brown and gave him a beer.

Everyone gathered in the den. Brown, who was one-quarter Cherokee, ran a hand through a head of thinning red hair and told Travis bluntly, "James hired me to build you a house. He's already paid me."

Becky gasped. Grandpa nodded with satisfaction. Echo wiped tears from her eyes. Erica knotted her hands together and hoped that Travis would accept.

"I can't take it," Travis said. "I already told him that Erica was going over my old blueprints to see how much the house would cost now. I can pay for it myself."

Erica found the councilman looking at her curiously. "I've heard about you," he said. "You fixed the roof on Sally Turtlehead's cabin the other day."

"She brought me some apples. It was a fair trade."

That wasn't true, and he knew it. The roof had taken all day and cost fifty dollars in new materials. But he just smiled politely and looked at her with approval.

"I can't take James's offer," Travis repeated grimly.

There was no arguing with him. Brown shrugged, finished his beer, and told Travis to call him if he changed his mind. After Brown left Echo said in soft rebuke, "Oh, Trav. You know it's not a handout. This is a family thing. Take it."

"No. All those years when he wouldn't come home, he sent money. I never took it then, and I'm not takin' it now. He's not proud of being one of us, and this is how he buys off his guilt."

"You're wrong," Erica replied. "You're still his idol. And all he's ever wanted was to make his family and his people proud of him. Do you know that he took steroids for years, just to be able to keep playing football, because he thought he had to be a symbol of what Indians could accomplish?"

Everyone looked at her blankly. No, they hadn't known, it was obvious. Travis's eyes narrowed in distress, and he cursed softly.

"Steroids?" Grandpa Sam asked, bewildered. As Becky explained what they were, Sam grew mournful. "He didn't have to do that."

"Yes, he did," Erica said gently. "Because he has so much pride in being a Cherokee that he wanted to represent the tribe the best way he knew how." She went on in a low voice, telling them some of the horror stories from James's football career.

When she finished, Travis was sitting with his head in his hands. Becky and Echo were crying. Grandpa Sam was fumbling with his pipe, his hands shaking.

"I'm telling you these private things because he won't say them himself," Erica murmured. "He doesn't want anyone to feel sorry for him." She looked at Travis. "Travis, let him build a house for you. Nothing would make him happier."

Becky went over and stroked her brother's hair. "Go call him. Tell him you'll accept his gift."

Travis got up and went to the phone on the kitchen wall. There weren't many private conversations in the Tall Wolf family, Erica had learned. So everyone followed him, including her.

She sat at the kitchen table between Grandpa and Echo, while Becky sat on the counter by the sink. Travis called a hotel number James had left.

When the hotel operator put him through Travis said, "James? Hmmm, sorry. Is James Tall Wolf there?"

Erica straightened slowly, her breath shallow. Who was in James's room? Travis frowned, glanced at her, then glanced away, frowning harder. His reaction alarmed her more.

"It's Travis. So you want to build me a house? Hmmm, yes. All right. Then I accept." Suddenly Travis grew very still and calm, as if having made a decision. "James, is there a woman in your room?" he asked sternly. "Stephen's friend. Where's Stephen?"

Travis looked at Erica and nodded solemnly. "When's Stephen coming back? Oh? Oh? Say, little brother, any messages for Erica? Yes, she's *right here*." Travis held out the phone to her.

James had a woman in his room, and his whole family knew it. Dammit, it wasn't fair. Now they felt sorry for her.

Erica was determined to sound normal. She got up, took the phone, and asked cheerfully, "Hi, Wolfman. Are you being naughty?"

He must have been embarrassed and annoyed by the whole situation, because it was a second before he managed to say anything. "I'm doing my best."

In the background Erica heard a television playing. Something with lots of car chases and guns, apparently. A woman laughed—one of those high-pitched, girlish, cute laughs.

This woman was definitely not part of the sound track.

Erica shut her eyes. If she got through this conversation without crying it would be because the shock hadn't worn off yet. "Well, I'm staying busy too. Sally Turtlehead is going to teach me how to make baskets."

"Good."

The woman laughed again. Erica dug her fingernails into her palms. To hell with being polite.

"You should have just told me about her, James. You didn't have to make up an excuse for going to Washington."

"She's my partner's friend," he said in a low, taut voice. "She's drunk. They stopped by here after a concert because she was threatening to throw up in his Porsche. He's gone downstairs to get a room for her."

"Ah. Okay." She simply didn't know what else to say. He was probably telling the truth. *No promises, no regrets*, he'd offered, and she'd accepted. So she didn't have the right to pry.

"Listen," he said, his voice hard. "You've got your deal back. The deal with George Gibson. I was going to tell you tomorrow, but I might as well do it now."

Erica grasped the counter top for support. "How did you know about that?"

"Stephen told me a few days ago. I talked to Gibson. He hired your old pal to take your place. Harold Brumby. But Brumby's in hot water with one of the unions, and Gibson doesn't like controversy, as you know."

James paused. "Stephen and I have some business deals with Gibson. We pressured him to take you back. If you want to accuse me of pimping for you, go ahead."

"No." Erica's shoulders slumped. He was simply trying to get her out of North Carolina as quickly and as honorably as possible.

"So take the job, okay? I've seen your work—I checked out the project that won the award for you. You won't have any trouble with Gibson, now that he's going to give you a chance. You're good. Damned good."

"Thank you." She couldn't have cared less about her work at that moment. "So I need to haul my fanny back to D.C. right away?"

"You got it."

"This ruins our bargain."

"No. You win. I'll get Dove's papers for you, and you can have her place."

"No. Only the papers. Not the home."

"Erica," he warned, the word full of tension.

But she was furious and heartbroken. She'd at least wanted to end their relationship in person, with kind, thoughtful words and a final kiss. Instead it was ending over a long-distance telephone connection, while some bimbo chortled in the background in sync with a cops-and-robbers show.

"Thank you for helping me with the Gibson deal," she said, and wondered how her straining throat could produce such calm tones. "When you get home to North Carolina just ask Grandpa Sam to interpret Dove's papers for me. We'll be square then."

There was a long pause on his end of the line. "Sounds like you're not coming back."

"Not for a while. The Gibson deal will take a lot of supervision. That shouldn't surprise you."

"No," he said softly. "Nothing surprises me anymore."

"Well, I've gotta go. Stop by my office in D.C. sometime before you leave for home. I'll buy you lunch."

"Lunch." He sounded bored, or exhausted, or both.

"Well, here's Travis again." Erica planted the phone in Travis's surprised hands and walked stiffly out of the room without looking back.

She went out the front door, crossed the yard, and leaned against the trunk of an old oak tree. Echo and Becky traipsed after her without the least bit of hesitation.

"What in the world was that all about?"

"You can't tell us that you don't love James."

Erica stared into the darkness of the mountains around them, thinking, "Let him be sorrowing as he goes along, and not for one night alone. Let him become an aimless wanderer, whose trail may never be followed."

She'd made a mistake by meddling with a Cherokee love formula, because it had worked only on her.

# Ten

The Tall Wolfs came from a proud people who'd always fought to protect what was theirs. If he let Erica Gallatin walk away without a battle, he ought to have his name changed to Worthless Wolf.

James got out of a taxi on the back street of a suburban office park and strode quickly into a two-story office building. He found the correct suite number on a list in the lobby, took the fire stairs in his hurry to reach the second floor, and went straight to a door with a neat little brass sign on it.

Gallatin Construction Company.

Let the war party begin.

A sturdy dark-haired woman rose from a desk in a small, plainly furnished reception area. She was plainly furnished in a beige suit, and she eyeballed him like a drill sergeant with a troublesome recruit.

"You must be Mr. Tall Wolf."

"You must be Marie." He smiled at her jauntily and sat down. "Is Erica busy?"

"She just got back from a meeting."

"With Mr. Gibson. I know. I arranged it."

The office manager glared at him. "I'll tell her that you're here. She may need a minute to call for the cavalry."

"Um. White woman speak with forked tongue."

Marie's eyebrows shot up and her lips clamped shut. She picked up the phone. "Erica? Mr. Tall Wolf is here to see you. Have you got a minute?"

Marie put the phone down and said primly, "She has just a minute."

James blew Marie a kiss and headed for a door across the room. Erica opened the door and stood there gazing at him, looking calm except for the bright blush her fair skin could never hide.

Wait. It wasn't a natural blush. She had on makeup, and her hair was pulled up in a soft but classic style, and she was wearing a beautifully tailored white suit with onyx jewelry and a black hankerchief peeking from the breast pocket. She was even taller than usual, in high-heeled black pumps that made her legs look about two miles long and worth every inch of the journey.

"I took your advice," she said simply, and waved a hand at her outfit. "I went shopping."

"Good Lord."

"No. Lord and Taylor. Come in."

He stepped inside and glanced around at functional colors and spartan furnishings that would have done justice to any finely decorated government office.

"Oh, don't worry, I'm having it redone," she said crisply. She settled behind her desk as James shut the door. His fingers moved so carefully that he knew she didn't hear him lock it.

"No more frumpy," she announced, gesturing at the room. "I'll change it all. Have a seat. What can I do for you?"

James took a seat on the corner of her desk, the corner nearest her chair. He drew one leg up, let the other dangle near her knees, and in general made himself provocatively comfortable while he watched a real blush creep slowly up her cheeks.

He loosened his blue tie a little, unbuttoned his blue-gray jacket, and flecked a piece of lint off the knee of dusky blue trousers.

"Blue," he said cheerfully, pulling his jacket open so

she'd get a good, close look at everything he had to offer. "In honor of your clan."

She blinked rapidly and made a great show of clasping her hands just so on her desk. Very impressive and businesslike, he thought with pride, except that she bumped a file folder and it slid to one side, revealing a very unbusinesslike paperback book.

James flicked a hand out and stole it just as her mouth popped open and her fingers reached anxiously for it. She pursed her lips and rapped newly manicured nails on the desk. "Do you mind?"

"*Savage Endearments*," James read solemnly. "He was a fierce Sioux chief, determined to take revenge on the settlers who had killed his people. She was a strong-willed schoolteacher from back east, determined to civilize a brutal land. But when he kidnapped her, she fell under the spell of his"—James paused dramatically—"*Savage Endearments*."

"There's a lot of history in that book," she said between clenched teeth.

James looked at her silently, sorting out his feelings. She was caught up in the Indian fantasy, then, like other women he'd known, and that was one reason she was attracted to him.

But it wasn't the only reason she liked him; he was certain of that, and so he could still hope. The best offense was a teasing defense.

James pointed to the book cover, where the chief embraced a schoolteacher so voluptuous that she was bursting from her low-cut gown. "What I want to know is, how come you never wore a dress like that to provoke my savage endearments?"

She took the book away and put it in a desk drawer. When she faced him again he saw a sheen of humiliation in her eyes, and it made his stomach twist with regret. The last thing he'd wanted to do was hurt her feelings.

"I brought you something," he said gruffly. James

reached into his jacket and handed her a sheaf of folded papers. "I checked on your great-grandfather. Here are some copies of what I found."

Her eyes brightened until she looked through the material. "It's true, then. Ross Gallatin was shot for being a spy."

"Erica, he must have been a very brave man. It was no dishonor to die that way."

"I know. I just wish my family had stayed closer to our Indian heritage. I mean, my great-grandfather Ross was a soldier, my grandfather was an actor, and my father flew fighter planes for the navy. I guess I don't have a very ethnic Indian background."

"Look what I got from the records in Oklahoma," James told her patiently. "Ross grew up on the reservation—no, I'm forgetting. It wasn't a damned reservation at that time, it was still the Cherokee Nation. A separate nation."

James pointed to a list. "See there? By the mid-1850s the whole Gallatin family was living in the Cherokee Nation in the Oklahoma territory. Justis, Katherine—Katlanicha must have been her Cherokee name—Silas, Holt, and Ross. He was raised Cherokee."

James added gently, "And when he died, at least he was killed by my great-grandfather and other Cherokee soldiers who knew he was a brave man and didn't look down on him for being an Indian or even a half-breed." He touched her cheek. "You've got a lot to be feel proud of, *kamama egwa.*"

Tears rose in her eyes as she gazed at him. James had to struggle not to reach for her. Patience, he told himself. In a good game plan, timing was everything.

"How did you get this material from Oklahoma?" she asked.

"Oh, I had somebody do a little research and send it to me."

She shook her head in disbelief. "Did you go to Oklahoma last week?"

"Well, I've always wanted to visit my mother's relatives out there—"

"Oh, James." She got up and started to touch him, then wavered, smiled wistfully, and sat back down. "Thank you," she said, her eyes brimming with tears.

James tried not to look disappointed. After the intimacies they'd shared, after all the long, lazy conversations and all the laughter, couldn't she even bring herself to hug him in gratitude?

"I wish you could have stayed in North Carolina a few more weeks," he said as casually as he could. "You really ought to consider coming back after this Gibson project gets under way."

She chuckled and swiped at the tears on her bottom lashes. "I have an aversion to lime-green motel furniture when it's in a—what?"

James had taken a handkerchief from one pocket and now dabbed mascara off her bottom lids. "You forgot that you have on makeup."

"Oh, hell." Looking embarrassed, she sat rigidly still and stared at his hand.

"That could make you cross-eyed. Why not look at me?" He arched a teasing brow. "Or do you still act wimpy when men admire you?"

Her gaze snapped up. "Is that what you're doing?" she asked softly, but with anger. "I don't understand why you came here today."

He put his hankerchief away slowly, as if thinking very hard. "I still don't understand why you lost interest in North Carolina so quickly."

"I didn't. You set up a deal for me. I have work to do."

"Once the project gets going you won't be needed on the site. Why don't you come visit the reservation for a few more weeks?"

She held up her hands in exasperation. "If you wanted me to stay longer, why did you go to so much trouble to get the Gibson contract reinstated?"

"I owed it to you. I was responsible."

"Responsibility!" Her tone was sardonic. "All you had to say was, 'I'm through being your teacher,' and I would have moved out of Dove's house."

"I'm not through."

She shook her head wearily. "Look, you're moving into Dove's house permanently, with all your personal possessions. You'll be making it a real home. So I can't stay there—"

"Why not?"

"Do you plan to stay somewhere else?"

James grimaced. What had happened? Why in the hell didn't she need him anymore, even for sex?

Frustration and distress boiled over suddenly. He stood up, planted a hand on each arm of her chair, and stared grimly into her eyes. "You wanted to learn everything," he asked in a low, seductive voice. "Do you think I've already taught you everything I know?"

"I don't want to play your games anymore," she whispered.

"You don't like this anymore?" He lifted one hand and trailed a fingertip down the silky off-white blouse showing between the lapels of her suit. When the breath soughed out of her, James slipped his hand under the jacket and stroked her breast.

The subtle forward movement of her body, needy for his touch, the immediate reaction under his fingertips, the shivering way her breath touched his face, made James sigh with relief.

"You'll always need me, at least in this way," he told her grimly, pulling her out of the chair and into a possessive embrace.

"James," she protested, then searched his eyes and whimpered "*James,*" in a yearning tone. "When you said you were coming up here and you didn't want me to come with you I thought you were tired of being my teacher."

"No, Red, Lord, no. I was only trying to do what was best for you. You've got me for whatever you need, for as long as you need it."

She made a tearful sound of surprise and raised her mouth to his, covering it with quick, tugging kisses as she stroked her fingertips over his jaw.

James bent her backward and licked her lips with the tip of his tongue, then savored them with a long, deep kiss that made her knees buckle. She sat down on the edge of her desk and he stepped closer, pushing her knees apart.

He'd known all along how he wanted this meeting to go; he was going to seduce her, court her, turn her inside out, until she wanted to be with him no matter what.

"I'm going to show you a new way to use your desk," he warned her.

"James!"

He pressed her down atop stacks of paper work and blueprints, his body covering hers. Her long legs dangled off the end of the desk, hugging his thighs as she struggled awkwardly for someplace to put her feet.

James parted her jacket and began unfastening the little pearl buttons down the center of her blouse, stopping every second or so to squeeze the incredibly soft hills on either side. She turned her head away and covered her mouth with both hands to muffle a soft moan.

The heat inside his body made caution difficult. James arched against her and asked wickedly, "How soundproof are your office walls, doll?"

Her chest moved swiftly. She was vibrating under him, her legs moving back and forth against his thighs, and it made him crazy with the need to satisfy his own wants, and hers too.

"I don't know," she finally managed to say, sounding breathless and distracted. "I've never had a business meeting . . . like this . . . before." She gripped his shoulders and looked at him with gleaming, startled eyes. "The door—"

"Is already locked," he said in a lecherous tone, and smiled.

Her lips parted in astonishment but quickly edged up at the corners. She yipped as he cupped both hands around her wriggling thighs and pulled them up to his hips.

James jerked open his trousers.

Erica yipped again. "You're not wearing any briefs!"

"I *knew* I forgot something this morning. We savages are like that."

She laughed helplessly. The sound broke off in a soft squeal of delight when he shoved her skirt up. His hands touched garters and, a little higher, sheer, lacy panties. She'd always favored plain cotton before. "More shopping," he murmured, with a hoarse chuckle.

"They're pretty flimsy," she whispered, and gave him a meaningful look. James sank his teeth into the shoulder of her jacket and hid his laughter there. With one quick motion of his hand he tore the silk barrier from her body.

"I'll replace them," he promised, and groaned softly when he saw the glow his impatience had brought to her eyes.

She gasped and moved underneath him, biting her lower lip to keep from making more sounds as he touched her.

"Just wrap those gorgeous legs around me and don't let go," James whispered, moving against her, then moving inside her, while her hands feathered over him and she lifted her mouth to take his in a long, sweet kiss.

He clasped her face between his hands and looked into her eyes. *Love me,* he ordered silently.

"*Da-nitaka,*" she whispered in a voice torn by bittersweet passion. "Oh, Wolfman, I'm so glad to be standing in your soul again."

Erica now understood exactly where she stood in James's soul, and it brought her a stoical sense of hope. Her lack of possessiveness had reassured him.

He thought that he didn't have to worry about hurting her when he moved to North Carolina, where he'd turn his attention to building a cozy, quiet life with some lucky Cherokee woman.

In the meantime, he gave her the kind of whole-hearted masculine attention that she'd only dreamed about. Washington was just a big playground to him, a playground filled with toys she'd always ignored in the past because she'd been too busy at work, and too self-conscious about going places alone.

But now she had James, who cheerfully sat through the touring production of *Cats* even though he said he'd listened to more interesting *wis-sah* music out-side his bedroom window when the moon was full; James, who introduced her to the joys of Sunday brunch, striptease checkers, *Sports Illustrated*, and the subtleties of the four-man defense as compared to the three-man defense with a designated nose-guard.

Sometimes they sat in her living room late at night eating popcorn and watching reruns of *The Lone Ranger*, and they broke each other up ad-libbing rude dialogue that made "Kemosabe" the only polite word Tonto said. Sometimes they watched old westerns and spent half the time yelling things like, "Call off the war party! They've sent for John Wayne!" and "Watch out, Running Buffalo, that white man's from Washington!"

Among other delicious secrets, they developed a game that when strangers came up to James in public and asked if he was Indian he feigned a blank look and Erica spoke to him in Spanish.

No, James would answer in horrible high-school Span-ish that he faked considerably, he was Rodriguez y Montasantonio, a diplomat from a small island country off the coast of Surador, in South America. He was in town to see the President.

She'd translate for the strangers, and they were al-ways suitably impressed.

Because James wanted to know more about the way

she'd grown up, she resurrected talents she thought she'd forgotten. She taught him how to fold dinner napkins into artistic designs, how to choose a good chablis, and how to do a respectable imitation of a Boston accent.

And finally, after he'd lived at her condominium for three weeks, he offered to show her his home in Virginia. She'd almost given up hope of seeing where he lived, because he seemed reluctant even to talk about it.

In honor of the trip he retrieved his car from storage at a Washington garage. She'd begun to wonder if he had an aversion to owning a car, since he always rented cars or took taxis.

Now Erica knew it was simply that he didn't need to own more than one car, not when he had the perfect car already. He drove her through the Virginia mountains in a mint-condition, cherry-red Chevrolet convertible, circa 1957. It was a lovely dinosaur that gleamed from the fins in back to the big chromed grill in front.

The car confirmed her suspicions. James liked a flashy lifestyle more than he wanted to admit, and he was going to have a hard time readjusting to the quiet simplicity of the reservation.

Then they arrived at his home. It was only a ninety-minute drive from Washington, but it belonged in another century.

"I told you it wasn't modern," James said solemnly, after they traversed the two-mile gravel road through dense woods, across a creek via a wooden bridge, to the top of a ridge, where Erica saw a small cabin built of hand-hewn logs.

She got out of the car and began to laugh. Even though she wanted him to be too cosmopolitan to leave Washington and her, she was so proud of him that she couldn't help chuckling at her misconceptions.

"A caveman," she announced, "would have found this a bit primitive."

James held out a hand. "Come see."

There were no modern utilities of any kind; just a well with a hand crank to draw water, a fireplace for heating and cooking, and oil lamps for light.

Inside, among crowded bookcases, animal skins, woodworking tools, and photographs of the family, Erica gazed in awe at magnificent oversized furniture ruggedly designed but impeccably crafted.

She stroked the sleek maple of a dresser and ran her fingers over the Cherokee symbols that he'd etched into one corner. "I know these. *Wa-ya*. Wolf. Is that your signature?"

James slid his arms around her from behind and looked over her shoulder. "Yeah. What do you think?"

"I think you could make a great reputation for yourself, selling this kind of furniture throughout the Southeast."

He chuckled. "You plan big. You think Becky can sell her beaded boots to Neiman-Marcus."

Erica nodded. Now seemed an appropriate time to mention her idea. "And I think if you were my partner we could buy up some of those shops in Cherokee and turn them into places the tribe could be proud of."

She rushed on, feeling anxious about James's reaction. "The two of us have the money to take a risk—we could bring in really topnotch Indian arts and crafts from all over the country. And why should the shops just sell Indian items? Art is art. We could bring in white artists too. You know, give them a classy place to show their work to an incredible number of tourists.

"You want to sell furniture? Sell it in one of your own shops. With a little luck and the support of the tribe I bet we could renovate the whole tourist strip."

James's hands tightened on her stomach. "And you'd want to supervise that project?" he asked in a soft, unfathomable voice.

Oh, damn. The thought of having her around that much made him nervous. He was afraid she'd want to stay permanently. "Well, no. You could supervise it. I'd be your long-distance partner, I suppose."

"Forget it."

He let go of her and walked to a window, where he stood looking out, with his hands shoved in the back pockets of his jeans. Erica swallowed tears of sorrow that had more to do with herself than the proposed shops.

"Why not, James?"

"It's a good idea, but you're the key promoter. I'm not a businessman—not really. I just want to build furniture. You're the wheeler-dealer. You're the one who would need to be in North Carolina all the time."

*Where I can watch you pick out a nice Cherokee wife and start a family? No, thanks.*

"I don't think I could live on the reservation," she murmured, twisting her hands together until they hurt. She loved Dove's place; she'd missed it more than she'd ever let James know. She could live there if she had work . . . and James.

He turned around, his face shuttered. There was no anger in him, or if there was, it was carefully submerged. "Maybe I can find someone to help you with this idea. Travis has a lot of friends on the tribe council. He'd know who to ask. But you really ought to think about getting a place on the reservation and living there at least part of the year."

"I'll think about it," she said cheerfully.

They stood there in awkward silence, as if neither of them had any idea what to do next. "Well," James said abruptly, "I didn't just bring you here to brighten up the place. Help me pack."


It was all over in a week's time. He was home, his stuff neatly arranged in Dove's house, *his* house, and Erica was still in Washington. She'd tenderly made love to him one last time and cried a little when he left.

He was miserable.

He was miserable, and on his first day home he was the guest of honor at a barbecue that seemed to have drawn half the Cherokee tribe.

"My grandson has come back to his people," Grandpa Sam said solemnly, gazing down at James from where he stood atop a chair in the front yard of the Tall Wolf home. In honor of the occasion he'd put on an outfit Becky had made for him—buckskin leggings held up by leather garters, a long buckskin loincloth, a colorfully striped thigh-length shirt belted with a braided sash, and a matching turban wound around his head.

That was the way Cherokee men had dressed in the early 1800s, and it had not only a certain nobility to it, it had sex appeal, James thought. When Grandpa Sam moved just right, he flashed a bit of brown thigh from under the hem of his shirt. The women in the crowd applauded and whistled. Grandpa bowed.

Travis braced an arm against Grandpa on one side to keep him from toppling over; Echo braced him on the other side. Grandpa Sam had had a few snorts of his favorite vodka.

"My other grandson has come home," he repeated, holding out his arms toward James. "Now I have all my grandchildren around me." Grandpa Sam grasped his heart. "As soon as they all marry and give me great-grandchildren, I can die happy."

With that announcement he climbed down and went off arm in arm with a small army of his cronies. Travis got up next. "My brother is an inspiration to me," he said, his gaze holding James's. "He's always tried to make his family proud. He's always loved his family and his tribe, and now he's come home, where we can take care of him, the way he deserves."

Travis got down, walked through the crowd, and hugged James silently, which was Travis's way of saying a great deal. After he turned and walked away, James stood without moving, his throat closed with emotion. If only Erica had been there to see that miracle. She'd helped make it happen.

He returned the tentative smiles and handshakes of people who'd never thought they'd see him and Travis as true brothers again. James was kissed on the cheek by a pretty young woman whom he remembered vaguely as one of Becky's classmates, and he was faintly aware of interested smiles from other women.

"Where is your friend from Washington?" one of them asked. "Are you going to marry her?"

"I'm never going to get married," he said with a devilish grin, and winked at her as he walked away. She giggled.

Two pairs of female hands latched onto his arms. "Now," Echo said sternly.

"Yes, *now*," Becky added. "Come with us."

They pulled him into the house and shut the door. Both of them put their hands on their hips and eyed him like angry chickens studying a fox.

"You can't ignore us any longer. Why didn't Erica come with you?" Becky asked.

"When is she coming back?" Echo demanded.

James was in no mood to explain that their big brother had fallen desperately in love with a woman who didn't love him. But if he didn't explain he felt reasonably certain that Echo and Becky would enlist Travis and Grandpa Sam and that together they would make him more miserable than he already was.

"She doesn't belong here. She knows that she wouldn't be happy here, and she's honest about it. But I'm sure she'll visit again."

Becky said something in Cherokee. He believed it was some sort of womanly insult aimed at him. "Did you ask her to come back?"

"In a way."

"Did you tell her that you loved her?"

"No. I don't recall telling either of you that I loved her either."

Echo tossed up her hands. "Are we blind?"

Becky jabbed a finger at him. "Are *you* blind?"

"No, but I wish I were deaf."

"Of course she won't come back if she thinks you don't love her," Echo protested.

James held up both hands patiently. "Now, sisters, I know neither of you has had a lot of experience with these kinds of relationships—"

"Arrrrgh," they said, more or less in unison.

Becky tapped his arm vigorously to emphasize her words. "Erica has too much dignity to chase a man who keeps saying that when he gets married he's going to pick a nice safe Cherokee woman who'll be sure not to run off and leave him."

"It's not like that," James insisted, frowning. "Has she ever told you that she loves me?"

Echo eyed him proudly. "She has too much dignity to talk about her feelings for you. I think she knew how much trouble there was between you and the family, and she didn't want to make any more. But we don't have to hear the words to know how much she cares. She told us about the steroids you took."

James stared at his sisters in dismay. "Why?"

"So we'd understand how hard you tried to make us proud all those years when we just thought you were a jerk."

Becky shook her finger at him. "Now, don't change our new opinion. Go get Erica."

About that time the front door opened. Grandpa Sam and Travis came in. "What's going on?" Travis asked.

"I'm being bullied by misguided sisters," James said wearily.

Grandpa Sam grasped his arm and looked down at him seriously. "Why didn't Eh-lee-ga come home with you?"

James shook his head in defeat. Surrounded by angry Indians. Now he knew how Custer had felt. He looked at Travis for support.

Travis crossed his arms and smiled pleasantly. "You're one dumb jock if you let her get away."

James groaned. "Look, she's headed for Boston right now to go to a party for her stepfather. He's just been appointed to the President's cabinet. As in President of the United States. You see what kind of life Erica leads? She's my best friend, but she doesn't love me, and she'd never move down here even if she *did* love me."

"I figured out some of that writing of Dove's you sent me," Grandpa Sam informed him. "And two of those medals of Eh-lee-ga's." He put a hand on James's shoulder and said solemnly, "I think you need to hear what I've learned." He smiled patiently. "And then I think you'll want to go to Boston and bring Eh-lee-ga home."

# *Eleven*

There was no doubt about it. James had taught her a self-confidence that went beyond the appeal of makeup, a new hairstyle, and a shimmering blue dress that left one shoulder bare and hugged her body from chest to ankle.

Something was different about her, whatever it was. Because for the first time in her life, Erica Alice Gallatin was surrounded by flirting men.

"Your mother tells me that you build houses. Perhaps we could have dinner and discuss an addition to my cottage at Cape Cod. You really ought to come out and see the place."

"Now you've given me proof—tall women are sexier than short women."

"I never knew Dorland Monroe had a beautiful stepdaughter living in Washington. Why don't you come up to Capitol Hill and have lunch with me?"

"The Boston Symphony's having a tea next week to honor a violinist from Surador who just won a big international competition. Care to attend as my guest?"

The attention had depressed her all evening, and the last invitation nearly dissolved her party smile.

Surador. The home of the great Cherokee diplomat Rodriguez y Montasantonio, alias James Tall Wolf. Erica blinked rapidly, made a polite excuse, and moved leadenly through the glittering crowd of gowns and tuxedos, feeling like a dark cloud surrounded by painfully bright sunshine.

She gave her empty champagne glass to one of the liveried waiters who was roaming the ballroom. The waiter had the terrified look all employees of her mother's wore.

Erica smiled at him reassuringly, but his eyes darted around as if she were some sort of spy. One false step, one dropped finger sandwich or spilled cocktail, and it was off to the dungeon—better known as the catering blacklist. Then he'd never serve squab au vin in Boston again.

Her beautiful, petite sisters breezed by, husbands in tow like cheerful penguins, all quite comfortably in their element.

Erica eased her way through the crowd to a distinguished, dapper little man who was holding court at one of the flower-decked cocktail tables.

"Pop," she murmured, and kissed his cheek. "It's a wonderful celebration."

Her stepfather looked up and smiled. "Your mother outdid herself." Dorland Monroe took her hand and frowned. "Are you having a good time? The Portuguese ambassador says you have an, ahem, 'alluring air of sorrow.' I suggested that you might have indigestion from the airplane food on the flight from Washington."

Erica chuckled. "I'm fine, Pop. Don't worry about me. Just enjoy your night."

She wandered outside, where the beauty of a star-canopied sky shone on guests who were dancing to elevator music provided by a small orchestra.

Elevators. Where were a private elevator and a big wolf when a big butterfly needed them? Erica bit her lip and felt the familiar anguish deep in her chest. She had a plan for learning to live without James. She'd simply move about in a daze and hope that no one noticed.

"There you are." She was grabbed low around the

waist by a lanky man who seemed intent on jiggling her with one hand and his martini with the other.

Erica leaned tactfully away from his campaign-promise smile. "Senator, I—"

"You're just what a politician needs. Big, strong, healthy, Republican—"

"Independent."

He was trying to dance, but his martini olive was the only thing keeping rhythm. "I like independence in a woman."

"Not that kind of independent. The political kind."

"Baby, I can be very persuasive—"

"Not with my daughter, you can't. Excuse me, Erica. Senator, please help yourself to the buffet. Immediately."

Tall, commanding Patricia Gallatin Monroe swept between them, a brusque referee uniformed in an Adolfo original. She sent the senator scurrying and faced Erica with a grandly annoyed expression. "A man wishes to speak to you."

Erica groaned. "Not another one."

"You should have told me you'd invited a guest."

"I didn't invite anyone."

"Then Mr. Tall Wolf invited himself, and I'll tell him you're not available."

Energy shot through Erica like a tonic. "Where is he?" She was already on her way inside.

"In the front hall," her mother called. "We really don't have space for another guest."

*Like a dead horse doesn't have room for more flies*, Erica thought ruefully, to quote Grandpa Sam. She hitched up her dress and ran as best she could despite spike heels.

James waited in the foyer, smiling with sly satisfaction because people were openly staring at him. His midnight hair and bronzed skin seemed more exotic than ever in the light of the foyer chandelier, and his big, powerful body was perfectly packaged in a sophisticated black tuxedo.

Erica met his dark eyes as she tottered through the

crowd, and he wasted no time cataloging every curve outlined by her gown. The smile that slid across his mouth said that wolves liked such goodies.

Breathless, Erica stopped at the foyer entrance and gazed at him in amazement. Happiness and bewilderment bubbled up inside her. *"Si yo, wa-ya egwa."*

*"Si yo, kamama egwa,"* he answered solemnly.

"I think he's from the Middle East," she heard someone whisper behind her. "They're speaking Arabic."

As Erica crossed the foyer to him she pressed her fingertips to her lips to hold back a smile that could too easily have accommodated tears.

Dangling over the lapels of his jacket was a necklace of wolf teeth that had been left to his family by his great-great-grandfather William. In one hand James casually held a leather bag covered with Becky's beadwork, and his feet were clad in mocassins.

"I'm the ambassador from North Carolina," he said gruffly, just before she kissed him lightly on the mouth. "I have a gift for you."

"James, you just went home yesterday. Why did you turn around and fly to Boston?"

His teasing attitude faded, and she saw the strain underlying it. "Because I know you're anxious to hear what Grandpa found when he translated Dove's papers and the medallions." James presented the bag to her and said gruffly, "These are yours and Tess's medallions. Grandpa hasn't translated Kat's yet. It's giving him some problems."

Erica clasped the gift to her tenderly. "Oh, James. You didn't have to come up here just to bring these to me."

He frowned again. "Well, it's my responsibility. I'm trying to tie up loose ends before I get too busy with things at home."

"Oh." Hope crashed inside her. He had an extraordinary sense of responsibility. Perhaps he just felt guilty for keeping Dove's papers from her all these weeks.

Erica straightened formally. "Well, did you just get here from the airport?"

"Yeah."

"Then come and have a drink, and something to eat."

"No." He nodded toward the bag. "Grandpa hasn't finished with Dove's papers, but he made some notes on what he's translated so far. She wrote some poetry that will, well, sort of surprise you. I can see that you're busy right now. Read the notes and call me tomorrow." He gave her the name of his hotel.

"Is that all?" Erica asked softly, her throat on fire. "You don't want to stay and visit?"

He glanced through the foyer and smiled at the finery and the crowd. James shook his head. "Not my style, Red."

"Not mine, either."

They traded a quiet, intense gaze. She searched his eyes desperately. "James, I—"

"Ms. Gallatin. Pardon me. Uh, pardon me, sir." A nervous waiter nodded to her, then James, then her again. "The senator asks if you'll meet him outside for the next dance."

Erica groaned inwardly. "Tell the senator that—"

"He can go stuff his ballot."

"James!"

Erica gaped at him as he strode to her. His teasing facade was gone.

"What senator?" he asked, glaring down at her.

Sorrow and confusion made a dangerous mixture. Erica retorted, "If you don't want to stay and dance with me, why do you care if someone else does?"

James grabbed her by one hand. "I've had enough politeness to last me my whole damned life. We're not getting anywhere this way. Come with me."

"James?" She teetered after him, clutching the leather bag and trying to kick her shoes off so that she could keep up with his long, impatient strides. "What's wrong?"

He halted, looked around, and finally trained his gaze on the winding staircase to the second level. "There."

"Let me . . ." She tried to get her high heels off before she broke an ankle. "I can't—"

He scooped her up over one shoulder and started climbing the stairs. Erica's undignified yelp brought guests running into the foyer. Hanging head down with her free hand braced on James's rump, she raised her gaze awkwardly and saw her mother gaping at her in disbelief.

"It's all right," Erica called. "It's a game."

James reached the second-floor landing and walked down a wide hallway, where the solemn furnishings whispered money and decorum. "It's not a game," he told her fiercely. "Not any longer."

He looked for an open door, found one, and carried her into her stepfather's private library. Erica watched him speechlessly after he plopped her on a massive antique reading table. "Open that bag," he ordered. He shoved the library door shut and locked it.

Erica fumbled distractedly with the leather sack. "Is it that important?"

He stood in front of her, scowling, his arms crossed, his legs apart. He looked like a modern war chief. "It's that important to me."

Her hands shaking, she laid hers and Tess's medallions on the table, then reached into the bag again. Erica cried out softly as she pulled her great-grandmother Erica's locket from the bag. It gleamed with a new covering of gold.

"Oh, James." She opened the locket and found the inscription restored. " 'Wed June 21, 1860. R.T.G. to E.A.R.' "

"I took it to a jeweler after I went back to Washington," James explained.

Erica pressed it to her lips and looked at him tearfully. "I'll never forget this moment."

"Look at Grandpa's notes about the medallions."

She put the locket aside and pulled a sheaf of type-written pages from the bag.

"Echo typed them for him," James explained. "His handwriting's not too steady."

Her heart racing, Erica gazed down at the first page.

Eh-lee-ga, when I finish with Dove's papers I think you and your cousins will have a good history of the Gallatin family as it was told to Dove by her father, Holt.

Some folks said Dove had powers to see the future. She wrote down her dreams in poems. I have figured out one that you will want to know.

But first, tell your cousin Tess that her medallion says on one side that Katherine Blue Song's parents and sisters are buried on the land in Gold Ridge. On the other side it says, "Katherine Gallatin, wife of Justis Gallatin. A bluebird should follow the sun."

Feeling awed, Erica raised her head and looked at James. "Then my Cherokee relatives are buried on the land in Gold Ridge. Katherine's family."

James nodded. "You don't want any mining company to come in and tear up that land."

"No." Trembling, Erica shook her head fervently. "Absolutely not. I'm sure Tess and Kat will agree that we don't want to lease it for mining."

He came to her and took the notes. After shuffling through them for a moment, he handed her back one page. When his hand brushed hers she felt the tremor in it. "James? Are you all right?"

"Read that," he murmured. "It's a poem Dove wrote."

Erica bent her head and read:

*I see the white butterfly surrounded by blue,*
*I see her bring light to the darkness,*

I see her welcome the cat who has a broken foot,
I see her gentle the wolf,
I see her fold her wings with contentment,
And love what I have loved,
Because this is where Eh-lee-ga the butterfly belongs.


Erica slid off the table and sat weakly in a chair. She couldn't describe the feeling of awe that shimmered in her veins. "It's amazing."

James knelt beside the chair. "A white *kamama* of the blue clan inside a house with blue walls," he whispered, his hand on her arm. "A house with rooms painted blue, like Dove's house. You put up floodlights so you wouldn't be afraid of the darkness. Your cousin Kat came to visit you with a fractured ankle." He paused, then added gruffly, "And you certainly gentled the wolf."

She looked at him through a haze of tears. She was crying from the wonder of it—the beauty of Dove Gallatin's gift. She finally felt like a Cherokee. "She even said my name. Eh-lee-ga."

James nodded. "And she said you'd be contented, because you'd be where you belonged."

Erica glanced away, swallowing hard. "I did feel that I belonged there."

He put the other pages in her lap. "Here," he said gruffly. "Read about your medallion."

She looked down, heedless of the tears slipping from her eyes. " 'I left my footprints on the trail where they cried, but I left my heart with Justis Gallatin'. On the other side of the medallion it says—"

Erica halted as James covered her lips with one finger. His gaze held hers desperately. "It says," he whispered, " 'A wolf will find his mate, no matter how far she roams.' "

She made a soft sound full of bittersweet emotion and said in a barely audible voice, "Do you think Justis rescued Katherine from the trail?"

James nodded. He gripped her arms tightly and,

ithout ever taking his eyes from hers, added, "I hope
 means something else, too. I think that's why Dove
ave it to you."

Old prophecies were a fragile bridge between them,
aiting for her to send them crashing or strengthen
hem. Erica took a deep breath. She would always be a
uilder.

"Is that why you've come here tonight? To . . . to find
our mate?"

Past and future were suspended as James searched
er eyes. *"Yes."*

She took his face between her hands. "Then you've
ound her," Erica answered softly.

The butterfly was content again, and the wolf was
nore gentle than ever. He lay on his back in a moun-
ain meadow, sighing peacefully from time to time.

"James?"

"Hmmm?"

"Don't you think we'll get sunburned if we do this
ery often?"

"Indian skin doesn't get sunburned," he answered,
ulling her closer to his side.

"Not even in delicate places?" Smiling, she caressed
he areas in question. "Not even on the *wautoli* or the
se-le-ne-eh?"

He chuckled. "I love it when you talk dirty." Then he
eached over and stroked her breasts. "Not even on the
ganuhdi-i."

"Ah. If you say so, then I won't worry."

He opened one eye and squinted at her in the sum-
ner sun. "But you're a different sort of Indian, so I
hink we'd better go back inside before you turn into a
edskin the painful way."

Erica kissed him. "Thank you, Wolfman, for understanding."

"No problem. I love your skin just the way it is."

She arched one brow. "Freckled?"

"Naked."

He chased her into the forest and tickled her whil[e] she tried to get dressed. When her T-shirt and cut-off[s] were finally back in place she attacked in revenge[,] biting his chest and stomach while he hopped on on[e] foot, pulling a pair of jogging shorts up his legs.

"Butterflies don't bite," he protested.

"When they're going to marry wolves, they have t[o] learn how to bite," she explained, laughing while sh[e] nipped at his shoulder.

He wrestled her to a truce, and they walked the res[t] of the way home holding hands companionably. The[y] found a note from Echo tacked to the front door. "Th[e] lawyer from Gold Ridge wants Erica to call him righ[t] away."

James stretched lazily. "I guess it's time we put in [a] telephone."

Still looking at the note, Erica chuckled. "Now, wh[y] do I suspect that cousin Kat has stirred up some sor[t] of trouble?"

"Trouble? Red, if you want trouble, c'm'ere." He sa[t] down in the rocking chair on the porch and pulled he[r] into his lap.

Erica put her arms around his neck. "I've grown t[o] love trouble," she whispered.

He looked at her gently. "Trouble loves you." Jame[s] touched the medallion she wore. "You stood in my sou[l] even before I knew you."

Erica nodded. "Katherine and Dove knew that yo[u] and I belonged together."

"Katherine knew?"

"A woman who'd go to so much trouble to preserv[e] her family's heritage must have known that it would b[e] cherished again someday. Maybe she was predictin[g] our future when she wrote about wolves finding thei[r] mates." Erica nodded solemnly. "I bet she and Dov[e] were in spiritual cahoots."

"Spiritual cahoots?" James repeated in a droll voice[.] "For a practical woman you've sure got some wild ideas.["]

"Look, if you can believe in Little People and invisible people who live underground and *Uktenas* and—"

"Then you can believe in prophecies stamped on gold medallions," James finished.

"Right." She touched her lips to his.

James leaned back and studied her for a moment. "Why, Eh-lee-ga Tall Wolf," he whispered happily, "I believe I can tell the future by looking in your eyes. And I love everything I see."

# THE EDITOR'S CORNER

What an extraordinary sextet of heroes we have for you next month! And the heroines are wonderful, too, but who's paying all that much attention when there are such fantastic men around?

Iris Johansen is back with a vibrantly emotional, truly thrilling romance, **MAGNIFICENT FOLLY**, LOVESWEPT #342. Iris's man of the month is Andrew Ramsey. (Remember him? Surprised to reencounter him as a hero? Well, he is a marvelous—no, magnificent—one!) When this handsome, unusually talented, and sensitive man appears in Lily Deslin's life, she almost goes into shock. The intuitive stranger attracts her wildly, while almost scaring her to death. Abruptly, Lily learns that Andrew has played a very special, very intimate role in her life and, having appeared as if by magic, is on the scene to protect her and her beloved daughter Cassie. Before the danger from the outside world begins, Lily is already in trouble because Andrew is unleashing in her powerful emotions and a deep secret she's kept buried for years. Iris's **GOLDEN CLASSIC, THE TRUSTWORTHY RED-HEAD,** is now on sale. If you read it—and we hope you will—we believe you'll have an especially wonderful time with **MAGNIFICENT FOLLY,** as Andrew, Lily, and Cassie take you back to Alex Ben Rashid's Sedikhan.

Ivan Rasmussen is one of the most gorgeous and dashing heroes ever . . . and you won't want to miss his love story in Janet Evanovich's **IVAN TAKES A WIFE,** LOVESWEPT #343. The fun begins when Stephanie Lowe substitutes for her cousin as cook on board Ivan's windjammer cruise in Maine coastal waters. Descended from a pirate, Ivan sweeps Stephanie off her feet while laughing at her Calamity Jane performance in his galley. He had never thought of settling down until he embraced Stephanie, and she had never been made to feel cherished until Ivan teased and flirted with her. But Stephanie has her hands full—a house that's falling apart, a shrivelling bank account, and some *very* strange goings-on that keep her and Ivan jumping once they're back on terra firma. There is a teenager in this story who is an absolutely priceless character as far as those of us on the LOVESWEPT staff are concerned. We hope you enjoy

*(continued)*

her and her remarkable role in this affair as much as we did. Full of humor and passion, **IVAN TAKES A WIFE** is a real winner!

Imagine meeting a red-bearded giant of a man who has muscles like boulders and a touch as gentle as rose petals. If you can dream him up, then you have a fair picture of Joker Vandergriff, Sandra Chastain's hero in **JOKER'S WILD**, LOVESWEPT #344. We can only thank Sandra for taking us in this story back to delightful Lizard Rock, with its magical hot springs and its wonderful people, where Joker is determined to heal the injuries of former Olympic skater Allison Josey. He mesmerizes her into accepting his massages, his tender touches, his sweet concern . . . his scorching kisses. Her wounds are emotional as well as physical, and they run deep. Joker has to fight her demons with all his considerable power. Then, in a dramatic twist, the tables turn and Joker has to learn to accept Allison's gift of love. As heartwarming as it is exciting, **JOKER'S WILD** leaves you feeling that all is more than right with the world.

Rugged, virile, smart, good-looking—that's Nick Jordan, hero of the intense and warm romance **TIGRESS**, LOVESWEPT #345, by Charlotte Hughes. What a dreamboat this sexy peach farmer is . . . and what a steamy delight is his romance with Natalie Courtland, a woman he finds stranded on his property during a freak snowstorm. The cabin fever they come to share has nothing to do with going stir-crazy as the storm keeps them confined to his home; it has everything to do with the wild attraction between them. Beyond their desire for each other, though, they seem to have nothing in common. Natalie is a divorce lawyer in Atlanta, and Nick has forsaken the world of glamorous condos, designer clothes, sophisticated entertainment, for a way of life he considers more real, more meaningful. How they resolve their differences so that love triumphs will keep you on the edge of your chair. A true delight first to last!

Ooh, la, la, here comes Mr. Tall, Dark, and Handsome himself—Dutton McHugh, Joan Elliott Pickart's devastating hero of **SWEET BLISS**, LOVESWEPT #346. When Bliss Barton wakes up with her first ever hangover, she finds a half-naked hunk in her bed! She could die of

*(continued)*

mortification—especially when she recognizes him as one of her brother's rowdy buddies. Dutton is not her type at all. Careful, cautious, an outsider in her family of free spirits, Bliss has kept her wild oats tightly packed away—while Dutton has scattered his to the four winds. When her family misunderstands the relationship between Bliss and Dutton, and applauds what they imagine is going on, Bliss decides to make it real. The hilarious and touching romance that follows is a true joy to read!

Fayrene Preston outdoes herself in creating her hero in **AMETHYST MIST,** LOVESWEPT #347. Brady McCullough is the epitome of rugged masculinity, sex appeal, and mystery. When Marissa Berryman literally falls into his life, he undergoes a sudden and dramatic change. He is wild to possess her ... not just for a night, but for all time. The confirmed bachelor, the ultimate loner has met his fate. And Marissa, who goes up in flames at his touch, is sure she's found her home at last. Parted by the legacies of their pasts, they have to make great personal journeys of understanding and change to fulfill their destiny to love. A breathlessly exciting love story with all of Fayrene's wonderfully evocative writing in full evidence!

I reminded you about Iris's **GOLDEN CLASSIC,** but don't forget the three other marvelous reissues now on sale ... **SOMETHING DIFFERENT,** by Kay Hooper; **THAT OLD FEELING,** by Fayrene Preston; and **TEMPORARY ANGEL,** by Billie Green. What fabulous romance reading. Enjoy!

With every good wish,

*Carolyn Nichols*

Carolyn Nichols
Editor
*LOVESWEPT*
Bantam Books
666 Fifth Avenue
New York, NY 10103